THE
BEAUTIFUL HANDMAIDEN
OF EVIL

Nordica laughed.

She darted forward to touch his cheek. Her hand was soft, smelling of that exotic balm with its awful overtones of rot. Her jade eyes glowed as she laughed at him.

"Don't stand in my path too often, barbarian. Powerful as you are, you might well embody the element of earth, the last one I require to close the circle of the four winds."

Her words were incomprehensible.
Elements? Four winds?
Riddles.

Author's preface

About a week ago, one of the guests at my daughter's wedding reception asked me a question I didn't expect. "What's happened to Brak?"

I was taken aback, but pleasantly so. So much attention has focused on the Kent Family Chronicles in the past few years that sometimes I almost forget that an earlier series of mine (and one of my favorites) attracted an audience no less loyal than that of the Kents.

Hence my pleasure when I heard the question. The audience is still there, it seems.

The gentleman who asked the question holds a doctorate in psychology—another nice proof of the wide appeal of fantasy literature in general, and sword and sorcery in particular. When I was reading fantasy works in my teens, it was assumed that only slightly daffy kids were interested in that kind of writing. Today only the uninformed offer such opinions.

It was in the role of dedicated Conan fan that I wrote the first Brak tale, *Devils in the Walls*. In spirit, anyway, the story was a Howard pastiche, and I have acknowledged the fact more than once. Still, as literary characters often do, Brak soon took on a distinctive life of his own. Sometimes the changes in his personality, story to story and book to book, surprised even me.

I put together this first collection of Brak tales in the late 1960's. Since its initial publication in 1968, it has never been out of print; well, not for more than a few weeks, anyway. I'm pleased that this Tower edition will maintain the continuity.

With a little luck, one of these days I may find time to add some new pieces to the canon. I hope the gentleman who asked the question would enjoy that. I know I would.

John Jakes

October 10, 1980

Chapter 1

THE MANWORM PIT

When Brak woke shortly after sunrise, he discovered that a strange thing had happened in the night.

For three days now, the land had risen steadily upward from a lush and pleasant river delta toward this forbidding region of gray slate, withered shrubs and distant thrusting peaks whose summits hid behind blowing clouds of mist. The land was lonely, as if nothing human dwelled there. The savage terrain suited Brak's melancholy turn of mind.

It had been less than a month since that painful evening in the grove of fig trees outside the great city. There, he had reluctantly parted from the beautiful, dark-haired young woman named Rhea.

Queen Rhea, of Phrixos.

It was difficult for the unlettered barbarian from the wild lands of the north to think of her in terms of her title and power. He had saved her from death on the infernal river Phrixos, then carried her away from the last of those who would have usurped her power by force. And in the great city, he had labored like a beast for her in a granite quarry. Bent his back for a six-month in order to accumulate the dinshas the metalsmiths would take in exchange for a great shield.

This shield, wrought into a symbolic design, he gave to Rhea. With it she could return to her people, who thought her dead, and convince them that she had lived through the ordeal of the sacred river and come back bearing a talisman of the approval of her gods. She could claim the throne then, and rule well and wisely—

But there had nearly been no parting at all. That night in the grove, he discovered that he loved her. He nearly rode with her back to her kingdom. The call of Khurdisan

7

the golden, his longed-for destination in the south, kept him from accompanying her. That and the knowledge that a queen could hardly share her throne with a barbarian who had been cast out by his own people in the north steppes.

So they had painfully parted. And he had ridden on to this forlorn, forbidding area of tumbled foothills where he woke to notice a strange and unsettling thing.

At sunset last night he had reached a fork in the road. One branch led generally westward, away through the rocks toward low peaks. That direction would eventually lead a traveler to the Pillars of Ebon at the far western ends of the known world.

The other branch turned to the southwest and the mist-shrouded scarps that were the beginnings of the Mountains of Smoke, eastern limits of the world and birthplace—so people said—of the various gods who held sway over kingdoms large and small.

Somehow during the night, that southeastern passage had been obliterated. Completely choked and blocked by an immense rockslide. Brak could see, higher up, the slate face from which all the boulders and rubble had sheared away, tumbling down to prevent any pilgrim from taking that particular route.

Brak shivered a little as he flung off the wolf-pelt which he used to ward off the chill of the upland nights. By a large stone, his pony was snorting and blowing gently. Brak patted its muzzle. He whispered soothing words, reached into the pouch at his waist for a handful of grains which he fed to the hungry pony. His eyes remained on the incredible jumble of rock. In effect, it dictated that he would have to take the western road whether he wished or not.

Slowly Brak ran his tongue round the inside of his mouth. He narrowed his eyes.

The rocks had fallen in the night. But he slept lightly in unfamiliar country like this.

Why, then, had he heard no sound?

In his mind he heard a voice and saw an awful sight.

He saw a man with a closely-shaven pate, aquiline nose, thin lips. The man's chin formed a sharp point. The upper parts of his ears were likewise pointed.

8

His eyes were huge, dark, staring, nearly all pupil. Little white showed. He had no eyelids. Evidently they had been removed by a crude surgical procedure. Light pads of scar tissue had encrusted above the sockets that held the eyes that never closed—

And the skin of that face was *alive*. It *crawled*.

Every inch of the skin was etched with tiny naked human figures, hundreds of them, intertwined and slowly writhing in postures of eternal torment. The figures were somehow prisoned *within* the layers of flesh and were crawling slowly there, crawling and moving and writhing in a never-ending pattern of bodies, arms, legs, torsos—

Abruptly Brak squeezed his eyelids together. This did not blot the vision. It was too deeply embedded in his mind. The voice, sepulchral, seemed to mock and taunt—

I will be there, barbarian. I will be there.

Thus had promised the Amyr of Evil upon Earth, Septegundus.

Memory of the crawling flesh of Septegundus troubled Brak's dreams much of late. He would never succeed in forgetting his first experiences in the so-called civilized world, in the kingdom of the Ice-marches, just after he came down from the steppes.

His own people had cast him out for mocking their warlike gods once too often, so he had been forced to seek his fortune elsewhere. He found the populous kingdoms of the world instantly bewildering.

In the Ice-marches, for example, he had first learned of the titanic and continuing struggle between the two great god-forces that ruled above all other gods.

Yob-Haggoth the Dark One stood like a black cloud before mankind, threatening the survival of all honor and decency. Or so said the Dark One's adversaries, those strange crypto-religious holy men, the Nestorians. In the Ice-marches Brak had been thrown in with one of their number, Friar Jerome. Thus he learned of the never-ending battle for dominion of the earth waged between the forces of the Nameless God, whose first apostle had been the ecstatic goatherd Nestoriamus, and the powers of Yob-Haggoth, whose deputy among men was the vile sorcerer, Septegundus.

In vivid detail Brak could call back the horror of the

9

near-sacrifice at the huge, ruined stone idol that represented Yob-Haggoth: a monster thing, squat and semi-human, with its stone fists resting upon the thighs of its crossed legs and its mouth turned downward as though to curse all mankind. At the base of that idol, Brak and the Friar nearly died as blood-victims of Yob-Haggoth, in an obscene rite presided over by Septegundus and Ariane—

Ariane.

Beautiful as Rhea was beautiful. Young. Creamy-skinned. Graceful. Mouth tempting as a plum. She offered herself, and her power and influence, to Brak. She was rejected. And in the awful cataclysm when Brak and the Friar fought their way free of the sacrificial rite, the barbarian maneuvered so that Ariane was between him and the whirling, enchanted dagger her father had thrown.

The dagger buried itself in the back of the Daughter of Hell, and the idol of Yob-Haggoth disintegrated in red lightnings.

Brak and the Friar and an old, blind minstrel named Tyresias escaped. The Friar begged the big barbarian to accept the way of the Nameless God. He tried to press into his hands the god's symbol—a stone cross with arms of equal length. Puzzled and angered by the ways of so-called civilized men, Brak refused the talisman. He went on his way toward Khurdisan, the far southern paradise where—so shamans told him before he was cast out of the north steppes—the cities were of gold.

In that fashion had Brak placed himself in confrontation with Septegundus and all the power of Yob-Haggoth. As he had ridden away from the Ice-marches, the ghostly voice of the vanished wizard had threatened him—

The road is long to Khurdisan, barbarian. I will be there.

I WILL BE THERE.

* * *

Staring at the mysterious rockslide now, Brak shuddered, wondering whether, at last, he was seeing a sign of the hand of Septegundus.

A soundless avalanche? Unnatural. Impossible.

Yet perhaps his imagination was merely conjuring fear-

10

devils. Perhaps he had slept more deeply than usual. He doubted it, but there was no way of telling.

A cloud passed over the face of the sun, casting a shadow. Brak shivered again. He shook his head and turned to his pony. He would take the only route left open to him. The westward road.

Chewing a hunk of salted meat taken from his waist-pouch, Brak mounted and started out. The cloud vanished. The sun shone bright as a metal disc.

The road wound this way and that, serpentine. The day grew hotter. Where the hoofs of his pony passed, dust whirled in tan clouds. Brak saw no other living soul. He had seen none for three full days.

When the scream ripped out on the low-moaning wind, he gave a violent start.

He grabbed for the hilt of the huge broadsword hanging at his waist. "That would be a human voice," he muttered to his pony. "Or is the wind tricking me?"

The pony obeyed the pressure of Brak's knee, halted. With his chin lifted, the yellow-haired barbarian sat listening.

Veils of dust obscured the tumbled hillsides where huge stones leaned at crazy angles. Presently Brak convinced himself that the wind had indeed deceived him. He didn't know the name of this kingdom, but he didn't much like it. He wanted to be free of it. He started the pony jogging forward again.

No doubt the memories that had troubled him all morning—foul memories of Septegundus, melancholy ones of Rhea—had filled his mind with phantoms.

High and sharp, the scream rang again.

Brak jumped to the ground. He left the pony standing at a bend in the rocky road. His broadsword glinted in the sunlight as he loped upward between boulders. Now he was convinced.

The scream was unmistakably human. Unmistakably female. And unmistakably terror-stricken.

He moved rapidly in response to the cry. The tail of the lion's hide which he wore about his hips flapped from side to side, matched by the swing of the long yellow braid that hung down his powerful naked back.

Brak localized the cry as coming from a slate bluff to

his right. The base of the bluff was concealed by the massive boulders between which he scrambled now. He neared the last rock rampart, pulled up short.

The scream broke out a third time, desperate, wailing. Brak saw no paths open between these rocks. He slammed the broadsword back into its sheath, leaped high.

His powerful fingers found holds on the tallest stone. He went scrambling over with a lithe, animal agility. At the rock's top he shielded his eyes a moment, a giant figure, wide-shouldered and naked save for that lion's hide with its long tail.

For an instant the barbarian wondered whether he'd stumbled upon more witchery.

No woman was in sight near the cliff base. Instead he saw a pillar of rock, bluish-colored, shot through with flecks of a sparkling mineral. The pillar was twice his height. Winds and weathers old as time had fluted and sculptured it into a peculiar shape—wide at the bottom, then narrowing until it flared again at the top.

Upon this pillar, cross-legged, veined arms folded over his spindly chest, sat an old man.

A coarse gray robe, tattered and faded, protected his emaciated chest and shanks. Little of his face showed. His skull, cheeks and chin were one continuous tangle of hoary growth.

The man's appearance tempted Brak to laughter. But two things kept him silent.

One was the object which the man wore on a thong around his neck. It was one of those odd stone crosses of the Nameless God, with horizontal and vertical arms of equal length.

The other was the man's face.

The old man sat with head thrown backward. His eyes were pressed shut. His lips formed a white line. He swayed, as if possessed, as if in a trance.

As Brak clambered down the face of the rock he muttered to himself. "What kind of trick is this? Imitating a woman's cry to frighten travelers. Or perhaps attract them? That's it. Probably there are robbers lurking close, ready to pounce on—"

Again the scream, blown on the softly keening wind.

12

Brak gazed past the pillar of rock where the old man swayed back and forth, hugging himself, lost in dreams or mystic visions. Then he noticed an opening at the base of the cliff. It was half hidden behind another jumble of stones.

But Brak was sure the scream had issued from the mouth of that cave.

Brak passed the pillar in great, loping strides. He spied a shepherd's crook carved from wood, lying on the ground. If brigands were setting a snare for the unwary, they were doing so with strange equipment.

Sword hand ready, Brak took a step into the dark of the cave. An odor washed over him. Brak's mouth wrenched.

The smell was the stink of decay, a green-black stench of primeval slime rotting away. The odor drifted from the dark ahead.

He heard the whimpering of the woman, steady and forlorn. Then there was another sound—the frenzied howl of an animal. Yet no animal's noise had ever sounded so loud in Brak's ear before. It hurt his head and set his heart thumping.

There was one instant when Brak's instincts rebelled. They warned him to turn and flee from the narrow cave. There was a thunderous cracking ahead, then an echo of it. The earth beneath Brak's feet shook faintly.

What lived down below? What sent up those bleats of blood-hunger and rocked the mountain with its thrashing?

Now Brak's eyes had accustomed to the gloom, which was relieved only by the dim light from outside. Brak saw that the cave angled downward until it seemed to end not far ahead.

With one hand pressed against the damp wall and the other tight on the broadsword haft, Brak crept forward. The roaring came again. It seemed to rise from the blackness where the tunnel floor ended. A pit?

For several moments Brak had heard no sound from the woman in trouble. All at once, as he neared the pit's lip, another moan reached his ears. Quickly he bellied down, crawled to the edge, stared over.

Far below, two great scarlet spots shone.

13

Eyes? Eyes that huge? In the head of what kind of creature? Certainly no kind Brak had ever encountered before.

Closer at hand he saw the woman. More precisely, a girl only slightly younger than Brak himself. Lying near Brak was a crude woven sandal with a split thong. Whoever she was, the girl had tumbled from the pit edge down a short incline to a narrow shelf. There she clung, an indistinct figure visible mainly because of the whiteness of her tunic and her face.

She had not seen Brak. She was staring down into the cavern where the red eyes smoldered.

"Girl?" Brak called softly, so as not to startle her. "Girl, look up here! I think I can reach you."

Her face lifted. Brak heard a gasp, a rattle of stones as her bare foot slipped. Rocks cascaded off the narrow shelf. Long moments later they struck far down, with dull echoes.

The girl kept staring while the thing in the pit flicked its red eyes open and shut, open and shut. It bellowed. The earth vibrated when it moved. Brak's belly churned with fear. The dead, decayed smell boiled up from the pit's bottom.

"Hold out your hand," Brak called.

"It's too far," the girl called. "I'm frightened of letting go."

"There's no other way. Hold with one hand, reach with the other."

The girl hesitated only a moment. Then she extended her right hand. Brak braced his mighty legs, stiffened his belly against the rim of the pit, thrust his right hand downward. The girl sobbed.

Their hands were a sword-hilt apart.

"Stretch on your toes!" Brak groaned with the effort of reaching. "A little higher—"

The girl fastened her left hand more tightly about the outcrop of rock she'd been gripping. Brak tightened the muscles of his legs until they ached, forcing himself forward another fraction, until the whole of his torso hung over into the blackness. Only the strength of his legs and the grip of his left hand around a rock imbedded in the tunnel floor kept him from falling. His long yellow braid

14

hung down past his sweaty cheek, tickling it maddeningly.

The ghastly red eyes, huge as midsummer moons, had opened again. They watched, watched from the black where the stench drifted. Out of the pit blew more than a smell. Out of the pit came some nameless, ancient evil palpable as a cloud.

Brak's face twisted as the gap between hands closed. Sharp rocks poked his belly, his thighs, little shafts of pain. His shoulders ached. Groping upward for his hand, the girl lost her balance.

She cried out. She started to fall. Brak thrust his whole body forward and caught her fingers.

Weight wrenched Brak's arm. "Hold fast," he breathed. "Hold fast a moment more—" For he had her now, had his fingers around her fragile wrist. What remained was the task of pulling her upward. He prayed for the strength to do it.

The girl dangled in space above the shelf. Brak knew he was hurting her. Slowly he began to tighten the muscles of his arm and lift her by sheer force.

His vision blurred. He bit his mouth until he tasted his own salty blood.

Higher. A bit higher.

Abruptly the rock to which he'd been clinging with his left hand shifted, torn out of its bed by the force of Brak's pull. Brak went rigid in an effort to keep from tumbling off into the pit. The girl's wrist slipped from his fingers.

For a timeless instant the yellow-haired barbarian knew that death was upon him, and the girl too. In the black heart of the earth where the red eyes watched, a roaring started again. A blast of welcome for the victims. The beast knew that death was near, too.

Then, as though some alien river had swept into his great body, coursed through it, foamed through it with new life, Brak's right arm began to shudder and burn.

Power filled it. Power so overwhelming it was pain. With a tormented cry Brak closed his hand more tightly around the girl's flesh, wrenched backward and up on his knees.

Blood beat in his temples. His eyes blurred. But his right arm was beyond all weakness, possessing a strength he dimly recognized as not his own.

The girl's head appeared at the pit rim. Brak risked freeing his left hand from its weak purchase on the loose rock. He caught the girl around the waist and wrenched again.

Man and girl fell in a heap, panting for air.

A moment later Brak rose. The peculiar flame-like pain in his right arm drained away. A tingling remained, as of tiny knives pricking the flesh. Then this too waned.

Meantime, the girl had risen. She stared at the vast black gulf just a step away. Then she faced around.

In the dim grayness of the tunnel Brak noticed that she was quite pretty. She had an oval face, a wide soft mouth and large dark eyes. Her brown hair, tangled by her ordeal, hung to her shoulders. Despite her youthful slimness, a womanly figure was apparent beneath the plain white wool gown held around the waist by a thin leather girdle.

The girl's face showed wonder. "I was falling. Falling to that—thing below. We were both falling, both lost. Yet I stand here now. And so do you."

A quizzical smile stirred Brak's mouth. "Girl, I'm as surprised as you. My arm is strong enough, but not that strong."

"Then how did you manage it?"

"I don't know."

A lizard poked its scaled head from a niche in the wall. It blinked, drew back. The stench from the pit began to sour Brak's belly again. There were too many mysteries in this weird hole in the earth to suit him. Not the least was the brief, inexplicable burst of strength that had surged into his arm at the critical moment.

He took the girl's hand. "We're free, anyway. Let's talk in the light."

Together they hurried from the cave. The girl's eyes widened as she perceived Brak's size, his girth, the savage cast of his features. His yellow braid and lion-hide waist clout flapped in the wind.

The girl's breathing grew more regular. But she clung near the wall of the bluff, huddling, either shy or frightened.

"I'm called Brak. I was riding along the road when I heard you cry out."

"From your looks, I'd guess you come from far away."

17

"The high steppes to the north. The wild lands. Leagues away. I'm bound south. Who are you? And how is it you came to be scrambling in that hole? It must run down to hell itself."

"No, only to the place where the Manworm lives."

Brak's spine prickled. "Manworm?"

"That is what they call it in this country. No one's ever come back from below to describe it."

"Something left from time's beginning," Brak muttered. "It smells that old, anyway."

"I did not go into the cave out of curiosity," the girl said. Her glances and her speech grew more nervous every moment, as if Brak's maleness frightened her. She picked up the fallen shepherd's crook. "My name is Elinor. I live far above, on those slopes." She indicated the nearby peaks. "I was raised by my father. He tended sheep, as I tend them now that he's dead. Once every sixth full moon I take them to market at the crossroads."

"A lonely life for a girl as young as you."

"The only life I know. It's better than living among the people, if the tales I hear at market are true. Anyway, this morning one of my ewes ran off. I followed her down from the mountain. She wandered into the cave and, as I went after her, fell to the Manworm. My sandal broke and I fell too. Somehow I landed on that little ledge. I was so terrified, I screamed and—and now I thank the gods I did."

Shyly she glanced at the big man. Her cheeks colored, as if speaking the way she had was somehow an immodest act.

"This country seems full of peculiar things," said Brak. "In return for my help, Elinor, will you tell me more about the Manworm? And about the old man yonder on the rock needle?" Brak shielded his eyes. "He's still asleep, it seems."

Elinor's eyes rounded. "Asleep or—venturing somewhere."

"Venturing?"

"His name is Ambrose the Pillarite. He worships some peculiar god that supposedly rules all the kingdoms of the world. But whoever heard of a god that could cross boundaries?" Brak said nothing. The girl went on, "Days

18

without end he sits there, dreaming. A market buyer told me once that Ambrose has strange powers. That he can send his mind wandering. Where, I don't know. Perhaps into visions."

Brak straightened. He used the tail of the lion's hide to swab some of the blood from his belly where sharp stones had broken his mahogany-tanned skin. He said:

"I set out not long ago to ride to the warm climes of Khurdisan far to the south, to seek my fortune. I follow the road where it leads. This time it seems to have led into a forbidding realm indeed." Distressed by the shepherd girl's nervousness, Brak smiled. "But it was good fortune that brought me past here today."

Stepping forward, he only meant to indicate friendliness. Elinor took it differently. Perhaps the initial step in claiming a crude reward. Brak sensed this at once, but it was too late. She snatched up her crook.

"I thank you for your bravery in saving my life. I will say a prayer at the grotto on the summit, to help with a safe journey. Now I must go back. There are wolves in the foothills, and the flock is alone."

"Wait!"

"No, I must go."

"Before you do, at least tell me where to find an inn—"

"Thank you, Brak, thank you."

The shepherd girl's cry drifted on the wind as she vanished around the corner of the bluff's base.

Momentarily angered, Brak ran after her. He caught a glimpse of her as she raced, fleet and agile, up the rocky hillside toward peaks where dark green patches of foliage shaded off to stone the color of pearl. The girl had a head start. Brak would never catch her.

With a muttered oath about the fickleness of women he turned around. The hairs on his neck stirred.

He was positive he was being watched.

Ambrose the Pillarite still swayed on his slender perch. Beyond the needle of rock Brak saw a dull wink-and-flash, as if a brazen helmet had been swiftly drawn back behind the cover of a boulder.

Unseen watchers? Another riddle! Brak had been exposed to enough of them for one day. He hauled out

19

his broadsword and charged up the slight rise.

Leaping around the rocks, he bolted into a narrow little defile. He was positive the watcher or watchers had been crouching there.

But the defile was empty.

Brak knelt down. He ran a thick finger over the hard surface of the ground. No trace of a human footprint. He listened.

The wind sighed. Above the sound, Ambrose the Pillarite moaned, and gave one sharp, painful cry.

That cry decided Brak's course. Perhaps he could waken the old man and receive some answers to his questions about this strange country. Not that he intended to remain long within its borders. But his curiosity had overcome him.

Tramping back along the defile, Brak became almost certain that he'd imagined the watcher. Doubtless the flash of light was the gleam of the sun breaking through the clouds a moment. Septegundus had said *I will be there*, and Brak had been troubled by mind-phantoms ever since.

Clutching his broadsword, the big barbarian walked down to the base of the pillar. Ambrose was awake. He regarded Brak with rather dazed amber-colored eyes. The eyes looked oddly young, bright, in contrast to the seamed face.

"So you finally woke up," Brak said.

The old man fingered the stone cross hanging on the neck thong. "Somewhat, somewhat."

"Are you wakeful enough to understand what I say?"

"Sleeping is sometimes waking. And sometimes not."

"Whatever that means. Old man, my name is Brak. I'm a foreigner riding through this country. While you took a nap, I could have used your help. A girl fell into the pit in the cave yonder."

The hermit's eyes cleared. They focused sharply on the brawny man standing below him. "Yes. The shepherd girl from the hills above us. Her name is Elinor. She was chasing a lost ewe."

"For a man with his eyes shut, you know a great deal about what happened."

Quickly the amber eyes grew veiled. "Don't question your good fortune too closely, barbarian."

20

"What good fortune?"

"Never mind. There is no other female in this district who might have wandered into the cave by accident. No one lives nearby save Elinor. Then since the girl in the cave was Elinor, she must have been hunting one of her flock. That you saved her by dint of your strong arms——" The Pillarite's gnarled lips seemed to twist in some private mirth. "—is also evident since she is not here, yet you are calm. You would not be calm had she perished and fallen to the Manworm."

The name made Brak completely forget to ask Ambrose to explain how he knew Elinor had been chasing a female sheep. "Manworm," he repeated. "What is it, old one? A serpent?"

Ambrose the Pillarite nodded. "Partly. Yet its brain is far more cunning. It's a huge, slime-covered thing, the last of its race. It's been alive in that cavern for centuries past all remembering. Some say the Dark One created it."

"Yob-Haggoth," said Brak.

The amber eyes flared. "You know of him?"

"Only the name," Brak hedged. "Gods don't interest me."

Ambrose thought this over, then said, "The Manworm is one of the reasons this land is doubly cursed."

Before Brak could speak the old man's eyes grew wider still, and he clutched his stone cross with one gnarled hand. "Take to your pony, barbarian. Mount up and don't look behind. Ride southward as you planned. This is an evil place, an evil time. Here, of all the pockets and crannies in the known word, the Manworm still screams and shakes the earth. Here, the murder of Celsus the alchemist has loosed havoc, and Scarletjaw as well. I fear the waxing of the power of Yob-Haggoth. Ride away, barbarian. Ride away from damnation."

The moment remained forever imprinted in Brak's brain: the old man on the needle-throne of rock seemed harmless and frail except for the amber luminescence of his eyes. Those eyes seemed to reach through Brak, and far beyond, encompassing all of time and many dark threats Brak did not understand.

Brak grew uneasy, suspicious of Ambrose and his ready explanations. The anchorite knew too much about him.

21

That he rode a pony. That he sought Khurdisan in the south. What was the exact nature of Ambrose's clair- voyance?

Of a sudden, Brak wondered whether the sudden, inex- plicable rush of strength into his right arm could somehow be connected with the anchorite's peculiarity. A manifestation of the power of the Nameless God? But Brak didn't believe in power like that.

Still, the strength *had* poured unbidden into Brak's arm. But where it had come from was a mystery. Had Am- brose's mind somehow——?

It was too cursed confusing. He shook his head. But his spine still crawled a little too, not in fright so much as in awe.

"I don't understand anything you say," Brak growled in near-defiance.

"Better so," Ambrose said, a trifle querulous himself. "Haven't I warned you sufficiently?"

"Old man, I'm not a child. I have fought for my life a hundred times. If the winds of bad fortune blow my way, at least I'd like to know from which quarter of the sky they come."

The Pillarite smiled wanly. "The sky? The winds? Odd you speak of them. In not many days, the winds in this country will rise. Rise and shriek and blow as they do nowhere else in the civilized world, Khurdisan included. They say *she* will call on the winds. That the winds are part of her magic."

Furiously Brak stamped his foot. "Damnation to your riddles! Who will call on the winds? That shepherd girl? And who or what is Scarletjaw you were prattling about a while ago? You said someone named Celsus was mur- dered. Now, be civil, old man, and explain these things or I might take my sword and——"

The mortal screams of Brak's pony tore across the jumbled hills.

The anger that had been beating high in Brak quickly waned. His cheeks turned white. He raced down among the rocks, broadsword whipped out of the scabbard and shining in his massive hand.

Bursting from between two boulders, Brak cursed, then gaped in disbelief.

In the center of the twisting road lay the remains of his pony, all bones and entrails and weltering, bubbling blood. The blood turned black where it seeped into the earth.

Distantly Brak heard a jingling, a bronze-shod clatter. He ran to the bend in the road.

A brazen chariot was thundering away, drawn by black horses and almost out of sight. And behind it lingered another stink even worse than that which had risen out of the Manworm's lair.

The aroma was a kind of warm, hairy stench such as caravan dogs possessed. But it was much more intense, and tainted with blood-smells. Brak knew then that some kind of dog had ruthlessly torn his pony apart.

But what sort of dog could destroy an animal three times its size?

No dog could do that. Not unless—Brak shuddered, hate thickening his blood—not unless the dog, like his stench trailing out behind, was of larger-than-normal proportions.

The dog smell, poisonously strong, drifted deeper into Brak's brain. The chariot vanished in dust around another bend.

Brak plunged back up the hillside. "Old man! *Old man!* A chariot passed. Some kind of animal—"

Under the fluted rock pillar Brak stopped. His shoulders slumped. Again a sense of impending evil engulfed him.

Ambrose the Pillarite had closed his eyes. He was swaying again and crooning to himself.

Brak shouted at him a while longer but with no effect. The shouts rang off the slate cliffs, unanswered. The sun slid under a cloud, and gloom settled on the day.

THE BEAST OF THE CARAVANSARY

After Brak gave up trying to rouse the dozing mystic, he unbuckled his broadsword. He slung the sheath across his shoulder and set off down the twisted road in the direction the chariot had taken—the same direction Brak himself had been traveling, before Elinor's cry rang out.

Soon Brak arrived at a crossroads. A peasant's wagon drawn by oxen lumbered by. The peasant informed Brak, whom he eyed with considerable suspicion, that a right-hand túrning would bring him to another junction. There stood a caravansary.

"The place isn't very crowded nowadays," the peasant said. "The traders from the isles in the Sea of Cham no longer send caravans as they did a year ago. Word travels swiftly when evil times come."

"What ails this land of yours, farmer?"

"Nothing I care to discuss with a stranger. Too free a tongue can bring evil spirits swooping down. Good day." The peasant prodded his breasts and the cart lurched away.

Puzzled, Brak strode on. The new road seemed more used than the one which twisted through the hills. Brak had emerged into a broad valley where the air was clear enough so that he could see the surrounding mountains capped by clouds.

Here and there in the valley Brak spied a lonely cottage. A woman gazed at him from an orchard, then made the sign against the evil eye and turned her back as he strode by with a long, loping gait. Even the fields looked poor. Perhaps at the caravansary he would learn what sickness gripped the land. After the peasant's cool reception, Brak had decided not to bother asking questions of the laborers he saw in the fields.

The oppressive clouds had cleared. The sun was sinking, red and swollen, when Brak arrived at the next junction. As the peasant had promised, a caravansary stood there.

The buildings were ramshackle. A string of tick-infested donkeys waited in the yard, where a dung-smell hung heavy. The drivers of the donkey caravan, swart southern men with curled beards and gold hoops in their ears, occupied a single table inside the main building. They swilled sour wine, argued among themselves in singsong voices and treated Brak to unfriendly stares.

"Will this buy a joint of meat, and wine, and a place to stay the night?" Brak asked the spindly innkeeper. He pulled out one of his last few dinshas from his pouch and tossed it onto the serving counter. The coin rang sharply in the sudden silence.

" 'Twill buy you half the space of this inn, stranger, since it goes begging night after night. Did you ride in? We'll look to your horse."

"I looked to my horse myself. I buried what was left of him on the road a good ways back."

The spindly man eyed Brak with curiosity. "You must be passing through our sweet land by chance, not choice. You're an outlander."

"From the steppe country, far north."

Brak accepted the goatskin of wine the host passed over. He tilted it back. He drank long and deeply. Then he swiped his mouth with his forearm, adding:

"This is not a prosperous kingdom."

"Aye. Once—little more than twelvemonth ago—it was fair and bountiful. Oh, not the richest land by any means, judging from what the traders tell me. Khurdisan far south takes that honor. But we lived decently, and with pride. All that has changed."

Brak's thick eyebrows knotted together. "What happened? Did a new ruler take power?"

"No, the same lord rules us. Strann of the Silver Balances."

"An unusual name."

"So called because he settles all disputes swiftly, and

keeps the peace through his tolerance and wisdom. But he is growing older. And his army is small. The few soldiers at his command are helpless."

"Why helpless, landlord? What's stricken this place like a plague?"

"Terror," whispered the innkeeper. "Terror of things unknown and awful."

Brak smacked his broadsword which was resting on a rough trestle table near the serving counter. "I've met few terrors this couldn't rout." Those exceptions perhaps being the powers of Septegundus and his daughter, he added silently to himself.

The innkeeper sighed. It was a sad, futile sound. "Try thrusting iron through a wraith. Through a witch. Through an animal with hide tough as—"

While Brak frowned, the man caught himself, shook his head:

"Ah, there's no use trying to explain the unexplainable. I'm no wizard. I know nothing of magic, and personally I don't care to."

"Magic? What magic?"

"The magic that lays waste to all our lands and even our future," replied the other in a dismal tone.

"This army you spoke about—"

"Lord Strann's. What of it?"

"You say magic holds it helpless? Holds your whole kingdom the same way?"

To show what he thought of that idea, Brak snorted.

The innkeeper glanced into the cobwebbed shadows of a corner, as though a threat lurked there. "You'd best not mock what you don't understand, outlander."

"But at least you can explain—"

"Other duties await my attention," came the curt reply. Although the bearded drivers who huddled at their table under one of the leaded windows had not beckoned him, the innkeeper hurried over to them anyway, and began talking in a low tone.

Brak slung the goatskin over his forearm. He sat at the table, uneasily. Being indoors still did not seem a natural thing to him. Confinement was alien to his nature, to the way he'd lived on the high steppes before he'd been forced to ride away to the more populous lands.

As twilight deepened to evening, he drank and mused over the landlord's cryptic remarks. The more he thought about it, the more the man's reticence annoyed him. He was ready to try questioning him again when a clink of armor and shields drew his attention to the yard.

A patrol of soldiers was riding in. Perhaps two dozen in all, they were a ragtag, dispirited-looking lot. The commander was a tall, stoutly-built man with a black beard. His trappings were in better repair than those of his men.

The commander ordered his troops to dismount. Murmurs of discontent, surly complaints reached Brak through the open window beside which he sat. The innkeeper hurried outdoors.

"Welcome, Lord Iskander."

"We'll sleep within your walls tonight," the commander returned. "Fetch a wine ration for the men."

"At once. Did you find the missing ones?"

Iskander swept off his plumed helmet. "No. Likely as not they all deserted. Rode up to her castle to offer their swords, I suppose." The man spat. "Even these fine specimens—threatened to mutiny if I forced them to march in pursuit. Therefore we compromised, and returned here for the night. Many more desertions and Lord Strann will have no army at all."

So saying, Iskander shook his head contemptuously and retired to a corner of the caravansary yard. There he sprawled to await the arrival of the wine.

After several draughts he closed his eyes. He appeared to sleep. Brak sat watching the troops whisper among themselves. In his travels he had seen his share of armies and soldiers serving various monarchs and potentates. But never had he seen any fighting men as demoralized as these. As the evening's gloom deepened they seemed to huddle closer together. They kept their weapons close at hand.

Finishing the goatskin of wine, Brak rose. He meant to go out to converse with the soldiers. He had just reached the doorway when the army horses, already stabled out of sight, began to stamp and whinny.

Instantly the commander jumped up. He pulled out his sword. There was a ferocious splintering of timbers somewhere. Then one of the military geldings thundered

27

into the courtyard, apparently having smashed out of his stall.

Iskander leaped out of the way. He was nearly trampled as the beast plunged on through the caravansary gate, mane streaming, eyes white and huge as moons.

Wheels creaked out in the gathering darkness. Orange flickers licked over the dirt of the yard. The firelight came from a pair of torches mounted in brackets on the rim of a chariot car.

The chariot wheeled to a halt in the gateway. Brak's insides tightened. Pawing and blowing, the pair of pure black horses hitched to the chariot stamped restlessly in their traces.

Several of the soldiers raced to the nearby stable building, managing to quiet the frightened mounts. The rest grouped near the yard wall, waiting. Iskander's dark locks shone in the torchlight. He too waited.

Several of the helpers from the caravansary crowded the door behind Brak. The big barbarian stared at the occupants of the chariot as they alighted. The first was a tall, slender young woman in a rich sea-green robe.

Behind her, even taller, and of rather cadaverous appearance, marched a man with a silver head cloth and a dark cowled cloak. The cloak's hem was stitched with silver thread that formed the various symbols of the natural elements, earth, air, fire and water.

Brak remembered having seen such a cloak in a marketplace to the north. The man wearing it was a member of the cult of the Magians. They practiced their occult mysteries in the warm southern countries near the borders of Khurdisan.

This particular Magian bore himself with a faint swagger. He seemed proud of his station and his sharp-nosed, sunburned good looks. Still, the relationship was clear—the Magian followed while the young woman led.

In the torch-glare the girl's hair shone like a new-mined wealth of copper. Her cheekbones were high, aristocratic. Her lips were full and red. She carried herself with authority, even though she maintained a supple feminine grace as she swept along.

Her slightly upturned jade-colored eyes, never still a moment, passed from this detail to that, from face to face

28

around the caravansary yard. Her glance said that she'd halted the chariot for the express purpose of calling attention to her power, real or fancied.

Her gaze swept toward Brak, locked briefly with his, then moved on. Just as suddenly her eyes came back again.

For a moment those eyes seemed to glow like chips of jade lit from behind by unnatural fires. A wave of nausea suddenly gripped Brak's belly, and a cloud of dizziness whirled over his mind. Perhaps it was exhaustion, or the rigors of all that had happened today.

The girl's eyes seemed to reach into the very essence of him. All at once he saw nothing save those eyes, burning like great consuming lights—

As abruptly as it had come, the sensation passed.

Somehow Brak knew he had been marked. An idea struggled in his bemused mind. He knew it was an idea of desperate importance. But he could not quite grasp hold of it.

The girl gave him a slow, lascivious smile. Then, breaking the tension of the scene, she caught up the hem of her sea-green robe.

The hem touched Brak's bare leg as the girl went by. There was a brief, inhuman sensation of burning. He smelled the girl's scent—a sweet, thick perfume that seemed to hold within itself a sulphurous odor of decay.

The cloud of scent settled in the air as the girl swept past Brak in the doorway, followed by the Magian.

"Landlord?" the girl cried. "Where are you? Stir your shiftless carcass!"

Immediately the innkeeper's piping voice replied, "Here, here. It is my pleasure to welcome you, my lady."

"But our pleasure," said the Magian, "lasts only so long as our patience. Bring us two flagons of your best wine. Plus chicken breasts, and a bit of roasted lamb."

"Lord Tamar," said the other man, "there is no spitted lamb prepared tonight. I—" He swallowed, wiped his hands on his stained breeches. "It shall be prepared shortly, as you command."

The girl laughed, a sweet, bell-like chiming. "Thank you, landlord. I appreciate your respect. That is why we go out for a drive. To learn who is respectful and who is not."

From his position just outside the door Brak watched the couple settle at a table. The innkeeper hastily called his staff together and sent them running into kitchen and wine-cellar. Iskander was staring at the windows of the inn. His lips were white. Hatred made his face ugly.

Brak strode across the yard. "Commander?"

Iskander hardly paid attention. "What?"

"My name is Brak. I'm newly come to this kingdom—"

"From where?" A cursory glance. Then Iskander's eyes returned to the inn building. "The north, eh . . ."

"Aye. And I'm curious about the man and woman. Who are they? Why do they frighten everyone?"

"Begone, outlander. I've no time to waste on idle—"

Then, abruptly, Iskander took a good look at the hulking barbarian. At the harsh set of his face. His powerful stature. His thick-muscled sword arm. The commander's eyes narrowed a little.

"On second thought, I'll answer your questions."

"Good of you," Brak said, a mocking grumble.

That managed to amuse Iskander. But only a little. His smile was weary:

"If I had a hundred or so of your size, I might not be standing here cowering before her. Should you be of a mind to stay on a while, there's a place for you in the army. A hundred places, five hundred! She's the one who has lured away half my troops, promising them wealth." As he went on, his strong voice seemed to carry an unbidden note of awe: "Nordica Fire-Hair. They call her a witch. I am beginning to believe it."

A scowl creased Brak's forehead. "Witch? She looks far too young."

"That proves you're an outlander. She's a hundred years old, a thousand, in terms of the secrets she must now possess. She is the only daughter of Celsus Hyrcanus, the alchemist. Ah—your face changed. Do you know the name?"

"I heard it only today," Brak replied. "From—one I passed on the road."

"The man, Tamar Zed, belongs to the cult of the
31

Magians. Eight full moons past, he arrived as though born from the air itself. Some swear he arrived on horseback, interrupting his journey to enjoy the hospitality of old Celsus. Others, equally certain, swear that he simply appeared one day with no belongings save those he wears on his back. Nordica, as I said, was the old alchemist's daughter."

A frown cut Brak's forehead again. "Was? Why do you speak of her that way? She still lives."

"Not the Nordica we knew of yore," Iskander answered. "Something has changed her. Poisoned her mouth. Her eyes. Her mind. A year ago she was a model daughter. Beautiful. Virtuous. Courteous to all. The change came over her shortly before the Magian arrived. Perhaps he caused her to become possessed. In any case, she and Tamar Zed formed an unnatural alliance. They sealed it with lust and murdered old Celsus."

"For what reason?"

Iskander shrugged. "Until about the time of his death, Celsus Hyrcanus was considered a kindly and harmless old gentlman. What magic he knew was not malevolent. Just prior to his murder, however, rumors spread that he had made a major discovery. After devoting his life to the search, he had at last unearthed the final alchemical secret."

Brak's spine prickled. "The secret of changing base metals into gold?"

"Aye. Transmutation. Nordica too vows it is so. She swears that she possesses the secret now. That's how she has been able to lure scores of men away from the service of Lord Strann. She's set them guarding her eagle's perch up in the mountains. And she's promised them shares of the gold she and Tamar say they can create from common lead. Whether they can or not, no one knows. Certainly the deserters believe it, and that's half the battle. As a result, the power of Lord Strann wanes. Fear of Nordica is everywhere. But whether there's a secret or not, I don't doubt she and Tamar murdered her old father to find out. She's changed, I tell you. Perhaps to a witch, as she herself boasts. She's become a curse on this land."

Before Brak could say anything, he caught a sudden whiff of an all too familiar stench blown to him by a shift in the clammy night breeze. The fluttering torches on the chariot threw harsh shadows on his broad features as he turned toward the gate.

"Commander, I smell something out of the grave."

"The animals in the stable scented it long before Nordica's chariot arrived. That is the real terror stalking this kingdom, Brak. That is why people hide in their cottages by day as well as night. That is why my soldiers yonder hang back. That is why even I—the dark gods curse me for a coward!—am reluctant to do what I ought. Run inside and spill her guts with my sword."

The odor churned around Brak, hot and overpowering. He saw a mental picture of his slaughtered pony. He began walking toward the gate.

Behind the chariot, chained to it, he glimpsed some kind of creature stretched out on the ground. As he drew closer, his brain struggled to comprehend what he saw with his eyes.

No dog on earth had ever grown to such great proportions.

"What is it?" Brak breathed, sword half drawn. "What kind of monster thing?"

Iskander had come up behind him. "A monster thing never seen in these parts, or perhaps anywhere, till Nordica underwent her baffling change. It too appeared one day behind her chariot, as though from nowhere."

Brak's face was bleak. He remembered the words of Ambrose the Pillarite about a double curse upon the land.

"Does the thing have a name?" he asked.

Iskander whispered, "Scarletjaw."

Scarletjaw. This was the beast that had slaughtered his pony. There could be no mistake about the evil reek.

Sprawled on the ground with its massive, blocky head resting on its forepaws, the dog looked to be half again as long as Brak was tall. Its flanks reflected the torchlight in a peculiar way, as gray iron would. The beast dozed. Two of its lower fangs protruded over its closed upper lip. The fangs were white, wet, long and sharp as daggers.

"She must be a witch, to create such an abomination," Brak muttered.

"Aye," agreed Iskander in a low tone. "Most times the monster is kept on its chain. But now and again she looses

33

it to amuse herself. Some dozen people have died from that kind of filthy amusement. Do you begin to understand why my men cower?"

Brak pulled his broadsword fully out. Red wrath was in him. "It's a dog," he said, "no more. It slew my pony."

Iskander's eyes flew wide. "Hold back, outlander! Its hide is like armor—"

The words faded as Brak loped past the chariot, sword upraised. The hound's eyes opened. Its great wet nostrils flared. With remarkable speed it scrambled to all fours.

Brak clasped both hands on the sword hilt. He drew the blade back over his head, then hauled it downward with all the force of his immense body.

Scarletjaw's mouth opened, displaying a thick, liverish tongue and teeth like rows of ivory spikes. Brak's blade smashed against the animal's side, hard enough to cleave a full-grown leopard in half.

Brak cursed. Pain flamed in his arm. The broadsword had struck and slid off Scarletjaw's flank as a rain-droplet strikes and slides off a stone.

Brak stumbled away. The unsuccessful attack had thrown him off balance. The hound's gigantic jaws opened wider, wet with slaver.

With its right forepaw Scarletjaw swiped at Brak's thigh. The blow looked almost playful. Yet it toppled Brak into the dust.

Scarletjaw crouched, neck-chain clanking. The beast's eyes shone a baleful yellow, watching the big barbarian.

Iskander's troops rushed toward the gate. The commander called loudly: "I tried to warn you, outlander! No iron can cut that hide—"

Scarletjaw lunged. Brak rolled over and over, trying to get out of the way. Scarletjaw was faster. It loomed over him, jaws agape.

Brak rolled onto his left side, swung his sword up and over with all his might.

When the blade jarred on Scarletjaw's armored neck, the jolting contact made Brak cry aloud.

Scarletjaw's cavernous red mouth grew wider, wider still as it retreated a few steps, then bore down on Brak again, ready to bite his head from his body. Brak had not succeeded in rolling far enough for the animal to be pulled

34

up short on the chain. And only that could save him now—

Wrenching his mighty body, Brak turned over and over in the dust, never releasing his broadsword. Then two sounds came to his ears: the protesting clank of chain pulled violently, and a woman's sharp command.

"Heel! *Heel, beast!* Let him lie!"

A moment later Brak staggered to his feet. His yellow hair hung in his eyes. His body was marked with dirt and bleeding cuts. Through a mist of rage and sweat he glimpsed a lovely face, and a darker, bearded one behind.

Brak strode toward Nordica Fire-Hair. She watched him closely, a mixture of rage and amusement and something else in her jade eyes. At her feet Scarletjaw whined and stretched out, its foreclaws digging and digging into the sod. The dog's strange, incredibly hard flanks heaved.

Nordica asked, "Where do you come from, barbarian? Certainly not from this district. Else you'd know better than to provoke my animal. Or me."

Still shaking with fury, Brak spat on the ground. "I come from a road, lady."

"A road?"

"A road near here. On that road this four-legged abomination killed my pony."

Nordica's jade eyes widened ever so slightly. "So you're the one. We were riding by, the poor beast was hungry and I saw no one who owned the pony." She dismissed the slaughter with a shrug which counted the pony's life a trifle.

"Then you can have no objection to my attacking your killer in turn," Brak said. He gestured with the broadsword. "These simpletons are terrified of the thing. Well, so am I. But I am a man. I'll sell my life like one."

As Nordica nodded slowly, her smile grew. And suddenly those weird lights were in her eyes again, shifting, coruscating, tormenting him with their awful, hypnotic attraction.

He was struck anew by the conviction that some important fact about this woman was locked in his dizzying brain. But he couldn't force the thought into his conscious mind. Instead, he felt himself being drained by the power of those eyes. He wrenched his head to one side.

35

Nordica's laugh tinkled. "Yes. For all your unkempt looks and uncouth ways, it's plain you're a man. There are not many hereabouts."

The Magian had been standing behind her during the conversation. Now he thrust forward.

"Will you let a clod like this insult you, Nordica? Turn the dog loose for a meal. Let the barbarian try his blade once more if he's so confident."

Brak glowered at the dark-cheeked man. "Perhaps I'll try it on you, charlatan."

With a curse Tamar Zed snatched at the dagger hanging from his belt. Nordica's hand whipped out. She seized his wrist. Brak saw her nails dig deep.

"No, Tamar."

"Damn you, let go!"

"I repeat it—*no!*"

Her face had lost some of its prettiness. Tamar flushed, bobbed his head to indicate reluctant submission. Nordica released his hand and said to him:

"Remember who I am, Magian. Remember what I own, and which of us is the master and which the servant."

Humiliated, Tamar Zed let the dagger clack back into its sheath. He peered at Brak over Nordica's shoulder, so completely in the thrall of the copper-haired girl that he would allow himself to be shamed rather than risk her disfavor. His eyes, watching Brak, were full of hate.

Nordica began to walk around Brak in a slow circle.

Suddenly he wondered at something Iskander had said. Something about Tamar causing Nordica to be possessed of devils. Could it perhaps be the other way round? Clearly she was the stronger of the two.

And yet that didn't jibe with the commander's statements about Nordica's model behavior prior to the appearance of the Magian. Some awful mystery was moving here. Brak thought he would be better off completely out of it.

But it was too late for that. Nordica was walking round and round him, watching, like a cat. All at once she stopped.

"I've decided I don't like you, barbarian."

"Nor I you, woman."

"I dislike anyone who stands against me."

36

His face remained sullen with defiance. Nordica laughed.

"But, as I said, there is a certain refreshing quality about your boldness."

She darted forward to touch his cheek. Her hand was soft, smelling of that exotic balm with its awful overtones of rot. Her jade eyes glowed as she laughed at him:

"Don't stand in my path too often, barbarian. I need only one more. Powerful as you are, you might well embody the element of earth, the last one I require to close the circle of the four winds."

Her words were incomprehensible. Elements? Four winds? Riddles.

As she stared at him, Brak's mind again fought to dredge up the thing which he knew and could not grasp. Her words played games with him, teased him. He was certain of it. Her words were masks behind which hid a truth she used to torment him. What truth? That was the thing he couldn't grasp.

"Somehow," she continued, "I hardly expect you'll heed my warning. In a way I'm rather pleased. In another—" Dark as emeralds now, her eyes mocked and mocked. "I pity your long-damned soul. *Tamar?*"

With the Magian following, she jumped lithely into the chariot car, seized the reins and wheeled the bronze vehicle around.

Iskander's troops scattered to keep from being run down. As the chariot flashed away into the darkness, Scarletjaw loped on the chain behind. Its hideous effluvium floated in the air like a warning. Brak watched until the torches on the chariot were fireflies winking on the plain.

Slowly he rubbed his forehead. It ached. The impact of Nordica's gaze was not easily shaken off.

Without warning, the thought that had been struggling in his brain emerged—

I have seen her before.

He scowled. He wiped his wrist across his sweating upper lip.

Seen her before? That was impossible. But he believed it. Felt it with harrowing certainty in all his bones.

He blinked into the darkness. Perhaps what he had seen

before was the kind of evil she represented. The evil of the Dark One and his followers. Nordica's eyes had conjured up an echo of that evil, that was it. If indeed her potential for evil did match that of the awful god Yob-Haggoth, then she would be a formidable opponent.

He was certain they'd meet again.

To her the life of a pony was a small thing, and therein lay her evil. To him the pony's life mattered much. His choice was clear-cut.

He would not slink away. He would punish her.

He was Brak, a man. He would punish her even though she might be able to call every last demon of the pit to her defense.

Chapter III

TOLLING OF THE DOOMSBELL

Through the night Brak slept badly. His dreams were bedeviled by phantom dogs with great red maws, by jade-green eyes, by the image of a bearded Magian's face alive with jealousy and wrath.

Morning was little better. A sickly grayness muffled the sky. Water dripped from the eaves of the caravansary and formed dank puddles in the empty yard. As Brak wolfed a butt of coarse bread and a plate of gruel he decided to set his mind to finding another mount. Just as he finished eating, the inn door opened.

Standing against the square of mist-blown sky was a short, thickly built young man with sunburned arms and a pleasant, roughly cut face. The man strode toward him.

Brak scowled. Was this some toady of Nordica's?

Outside, in the mud, Brak glimpsed a mangy donkey and a fine mahogany-colored pony with a tooled saddle decorated with silver bosses. The lop-eared ass suited the peasant's coarse clothes and appearance as exactly as the horse did not.

The new arrival stopped in front of Brak and hooked his thumbs in his rope belt. "Since you appear to be the only stranger on the premises, you must be the outlander. The one who attacked Nordica's hound."

Brak nodded in a surly way, unsure of the man's intentions. "The thing killed my pony."

"I come from the palace of Strann, Lord of the Silver Balances. To make amends, if that's possible."

A disgusted snort waas Brak's reply. "Why? The beast got the better of me."

"At least you had the courage to stand up to Nordica. Not many do these days. I am pleased to meet a man who regards her as I do—as a curse and abomination."

For the first time that morning, Brak was amused. He laughed loudly. "They surely don't know your value at the palace, fellow. For a servant, you're outspoken."

Now it was the stocky man's turn to show amusement. "I am a servant of one person only, Brak. I understand that's how you're called. I obey no one but my father Strann."

The gruel bowl tumbled out of Brak's hand and dumped on the floor. He gaped at the man's poor garments.

"You—the lord's son?"

"Aye. Pemma is my name. Prince Pemma, to be stuffy about it. Frankly I don't put much stock in titles especially in grim times like these."

Without ceremony Pemma hooked his sandal around the leg of a stool. He pulled the stool from under the table and sat down. The red in Brak's cheeks receded slowly.

"Word of what happened here last night reached my father swiftly, Brak. Iskander marched back to the palace before dawn in order to re-provision, you see . . ."

The barbarian nodded. "I noticed earlier that the soldiers had gone."

"Aye. The moment Lord Strann got the news about you, he woke me up and bade me bring the finest pony left in our stables, as well as gear. My father requests that you ride up to the palace. He wishes to thank you himself. The pony, food, lodging—all yours if you want it. Perhaps we might even persuade you to stay a while." Pemma's eyes had grown grim. "We need brave men."

The barbarian nodded. "That seems plain. But the problem is not one of courage alone. Even brave men are hard pressed to stand against magic."

"True enough. But still, the effort counts for half the war. Some are no longer even willing to try." He paused. "Are you?"

"Yes," Brak answered without hesitating. "The woman needs to be taught a lesson. I'm not a man of great wits, Prince. Nor do I understand much of spells and sorcery, though I have encountered such before. But on the high steppes where I was born, the slayer of a man's pony is caught and quartered. Killing a man's horse is held to be akin to chopping off his legs."

"Well put. Will you accept my father's hospitality? And the pony?"

Brak rose. "I will."

Together the two men left the caravansary. They set off along the highroad that sloped up to the foothills of the mountains. As they jogged along, Pemma pointed to laborers tilling the fields with crude implements.

"These lands belong to my father. I am his overseer. 'Tis a lowly occupation for a king's son, I suppose. But when I was young and this land was happier, Strann taught me to love the soil, the miracle of growing things. To this day I prefer to have my hands in black loam rather than around the hilt of a sword."

Brak studied the workers bent over their tasks in the fields. "Your crops look poor. Is that the witch-girl's doing too?"

"In part. Our crops fail because our spirits do likewise."

"Is Nordica really that bad?"

"Worse. It wasn't always so."

At this Brak nodded. "I heard the tale last night at the inn. A model daughter, Iskander called her."

"Until Hell or Tamar Zed or both made her a changeling," Pemma agreed. "There is something foul and unearthly in the way the transformation took place. So quickly, so completely! Then there's that abominable hound. Out of nowhere! Perhaps it all has something to do with the tales that she worships some sort of beastly god."

A chill prickled Brak's spine. "What kind of god might that be?"

"None of our local deities, for certain," Prince Pemma frowned. "They're all fat-bellied winebibbers. The only thing our gods would hurt is the skin of a grape, in order to get at the juice inside. No, it must be some strange, malevolent god. I don't know its name. Nor do I even know whether the tales that Nordica does homage to it are true. We need not becloud matters by discussing it, really. Things are dark enough as it is. We need no intervention of blasphemous powers to make them even darker."

The big barbarian's eyes brooded on the roadway ahead. In his mind he saw the blind stone eyes of the Yob-Haggoth, and heard again the warning voice of the Nestorian Friar, Jerome, as clearly as though the horror that had transpired in the Ice-marches had taken place only the preceding day:

Each kingdom and principality of this world is ruled by its own god or gods. Some are powerful, with many spells and wizardries at their command. Yet most mighty of all are the two who constantly war for ultimate supremacy. Their presence is, for the most part, undreamed of by the lords and princes and commoners and magi who keep their eyes focused upon smaller, meaner matters, smaller, meaner gods.

Centuries in the past, before the Scroll of History was even a little way unrolled, one of these two powerful gods ruled all the world, and his baleful image was worshipped in loathesome rites. That worship has been banished many years. But he has not died. He only slumbers.

And of late, there are signs, the Friar said with dolorous mien, *that Yob-Haggoth has reasserted his power——*

To claim Nordica Fire-Hair as one of his disciples? Brak wondered.

Certainly something must account for the weird, preternatural power of her jade eyes, as well as for the fact that

41

he believed he had encountered her before. Perhaps what he saw in her gaze was the reflection of Yob-Haggoth's resurrected evil.

A disturbing thought. And one which he didn't care to discuss with the prince. He had too little evidence for his suspicion. Instead, he asked:

"Isn't it possible for your father to come to terms with Nordica?"

Surprised, Pemma looked hard at Brak. "Would you come to terms after what her dog did to your pony?"

"Never, Pemma. But you're a king's son. The king must protect his people."

"If Nordica has her way," Pemma said, "she'll soon replace my father as the power in this country. When her father was alive, no one feared the occult secrets that, so it was said, had been in his family generation upon generation. Celsus Hyrcanus was a man who burned with the desire to know, to understand. But he was not cruel. And had no designs on the throne. He spent most of his life hunting the ultimate alchemical formula only so he might savor the satisfaction of having discovered it. Celsus even promised Lord Strann that he would turn the secret over to him if he ever found it. Celsus wished the entire kingdom to prosper. Then the Magian came, Nordica changed, and old Celsus vanished. I'm sure they killed him. Killed him . . . or worse."

Pemma's donkey had stopped next to a league marker at the roadside. Beside the small stone pyramid a road branched off to the fields.

"Perhaps," Pemma mused, "the spirit of Celsus Hyrcanus is still alive in Hell, or somewhere else."

"How did he die?" Brak asked.

"No one knows."

"He simply disappeared?"

"Yes."

Brak's forehead furrowed. "And Nordica possesses his secret?"

"Again, no one is positive. I can see no other reason for the sudden vanishing—death—of her father. She vows she has the formula. But she's yet to put it to use. No fresh-minted bullion has appeared in the markets. The soldiers who have deserted to her are paid with hope and promises

42

alone. Well—I must leave you here, Brak, and go tend the affairs of the land. Ride on up this road. You'll soon see the palace. Perhaps, when we meet tonight at table, between us we can think of some way to strike Nordica Fire-Hair. Each of us in his own way, I think, would like to see her fall."

Brak nodded. "To the bottom of the world would not be far enough."

Prince Pemma laughed, signaled to his animal and jogged off along the side road, which led to a vast area of grape arbors. Brak drew his wolf-pelt cloak tightly around his shoulders. The mist had grown heavier. He kneed the pony forward.

The horse Pemma had provided pleased Brak. The little animal seemed sure of foot, with a friskiness that suggested speed and stamina. Riding along, Brak's mood improved. As the road slanted upward, he strained forward, searching the horizon for the palace.

Presently he saw battlements rising up against the slate-colored sky. Above a mighty gate rose a tall, square tower. Inside the tower hung a huge bell. Two guards stood shivering in the mist just inside the gate through which Brak clattered after crossing a moat bridge. Except for those men, plus the single curl of smoke rising from one outbuilding, the many-winged palace of Lord Strann looked deserted.

Scabbard slung across his shoulder, Brak strode up broad stairs. Another guard materialized from a gloomy cloister. He gave the big barbarian directions to the central chamber.

After passing many deserted rooms that were nearly bare of furnishings, Brak reached a vaulted hall. At one end, high silver doors opened onto a larger room beyond.

Listless guards in threadbare trappings leaned on their spears at the main doors. Above the door arch a silver scale with its pans level was worked into the masonry. As Brak passed beneath the arch he noticed that flakes of the silverwork had dropped off in many places. Indeed the entire palace had a scabrous, decrepit look. As though it were dying.

Brak marched across the cracked marble flooring of the

43

audience hall toward the man waiting on the dais.

The man wore purple robes. Once they had been rich. Now they were faded. The man's beard was silver, like the balances above the portal. His handsome face was shrunken, pale. He lay on a couch. As he attempted to lift himself at Brak's approach, he groaned low in pain.

Drawing closer, Brak saw how really ill the man looked, stretched out there on his side, with one limp hand holding a parchment. At the lord's feet a dwarf in ragged motley snored. Otherwise Strann was unattended.

"My name is Brak, Lord. I was sent here by your son, Prince Pemma."

Strann nodded. The determined, almost feverish dark eyes did not match the rest of his wasted appearance.

"Welcome, Brak. I trust no one tried to bar your way."

"No one, Lord."

"Not that we have a great many householders to do so any more. Hardly even enough to keep the fires banked." He gestured to a huge hearth where embers glowed. There was no hint of self-pity in Strann's speech. Merely the statement of inevitable fact. "Sit here at my feet, Brak, while I have wine fetched for us."

Strann tweaked the dwarf's shoulder. The little man awoke and Strann sent him scuttling off. Then he continued:

"The story of how you attacked Scarletjaw reached me through Iskander early today."

"So your son said, Lord."

"I felt that such bravery should be rewarded."

"Bravery seems of little use against the witch-woman."

"That's true. Though Nordica Fire-Hair is mortal, the sources of her sudden power are beyond the ken of most mortal minds. I lie here hour after hour dreaming of ways to thwart her before she seduces all my people with her promises. It's useless. I have no way to counteract her magic. I am not even strong enough to take up a sword against her. The physicians tell me that my infirmity is merely the advent of old age. Perhaps so. My legs refuse to obey me. My sight fails at times. But my will remains strong. And my will dictates my sole strong wish—to destroy Nordica and the slavering thing that guards her."

45

Strann reached for the jar of wine the dwarf had deposited on the dais. His expression grew sad all at once. Brak was angered to see such a fine, warlike face destroyed by age and sickness and fear.

"Surely," Brak said, "there is a way to kill the beast." Brak spoke as the dwarf poured him a cup of sweet wine. "Surely something will destroy it.'"

Strann raised on an elbow. "Is that why you accepted my invitation, outlander? Because you want to fight?"

Brak nodded. "Your quarrel is none of mine. That is, it wasn't when I rode into your country. But what happened yesterday, on the road and at the caravansary, has made it my quarrel."

The ruler chuckled feebly. "Welcome news."

"I have no magical skills, Lord. Only a right arm and a sword."

"And courage! My son Pemma has that too, in full measure. But he lacks the physical stature of a warrior. Perhaps you and Iskander can conceive a plan—" Strann shook his head. "Forgive me. No doubt you're weary. Tonight at dinner we'll turn our thoughts to Nordica. For the moment, tell me more about yourself. Where you're from and where you're bound."

The yellow-haired barbarian proceeded to describe a number of the adventures which had befallen him since leaving his homeland in the north. He did not dwell over-long on the harrowing story of his encounter with Septegundus in the Ice-marches. Nor did he mention the wizard's repeated warning that he would bar Brak's path to the south. There was no point in telling Lord Strann about personal circumstances which might or might not have a bearing on the future.

When he described how he had come into Strann's kingdom, however—taking a road he had no choice but to follow—the lord's eyes gleamed with interest.

"It is almost as though your coming here was ordained," Strann commented.

"I prefer to consider it just a turn of chance," Brak replied, without real conviction.

Strann seemed to retreat into a reverie. He roused from it a moment later, managed a feeble smile.

46

"A most colorful and interesting recital, Brak. But I fear I've kept you talking too long, and given you too little chance to refresh yourself."

Brak eyed the platter of joints of cold meat which the dwarf had fetched some time ago. Strann nodded.

"No more conversation, then. Eat your fill."

With great gulps and snarls, Brak tore into the succulent joints. Strann smiled with gentle amusement.

Brak cared little about the spectacle he made. He was ravenous. And it was satisfying to engage in the normal human act of eating, when most everything else in this land seemed so abnormal.

Just as the big barbarian was washing down the last of the meat with huge swallows of wine, the air reverberated with a heavy, mournful clanging.

Strann went rigid on his couch. His right hand twitched, knocking aside a wine jar. It broke noisily, spilling the wine on the marble like blood.

"The doomsbell," Strann whispered. "Over the gate——"

Brak jumped to his feet. "What does it signal? An attack?"

"They ring it only when there is disaster in the fields."

"Your son!" Brak exclaimed. "Lord, I'll go."

"Yes, and swiftly. The soldiers are timid and slow."

Whirling, Brak rushed from the chamber. He raced down through the great moldering rooms of the royal house and out into the yard where his pony waited. A small troop of Strann's household guards had already assembled. But the soldiers seemed to be having trouble readying their horses and fastening their saddles.

The barbarian hauled himself up on his pony as the mighty bell swung slowly, slowly back and forth. Its clapper struck the rim with a brazen thunder that hurt Brak's eardrums.

Flashing through the gate at a gallop, he saw one of the guards hauling on the bell-rope. The man was trembling.

Wind and mist stung Brak's cheeks as he thundered down the highroad. His lion-tail and his yellow braid stood out straight behind. He craned forward in the saddle, searching the mist for the source of the alarm.

Suddenly he spied a man lying half-dazed in a ditch.

The man's head was cracked open. Blood dripped black down his cheek. Brak reined hard.

"Why is the bell ringing?" he shouted. "What happened in the field?"

"Pemma needs help," the man gasped, rising on one elbow, white-faced. "Are you the only one who's come from the palace? *Where are the rest?*"

Brak tore the broadsword from its scabbard and leaned out of the saddle. His face was ugly.

"Speak sense, fellow, or I'll lop your head clean off. What's happened?"

"Soldiers," the peasant cried. "Strann's once but—now they're Nordica's."

With his spindly hand he pointed into the mist-shrouded fields. Faintly Brak heard steel ringing on steel, and shouts.

"Yonder," the man went on. "Past the league marker in—in the grape arbors. Nordica's soldiers are hunting the prince—"

Brak jerked the pony's head around and sent him flying down the road.

As Brak thundered up to the marker stone and swung to the right, into the fields, the sound of fighting grew louder. Women's screams drifted to his ears, and the heavy thud of hoofs.

He galloped down the side road. Eerie shapes loomed out of the mist ahead—horsemen armed with swords and spears, some carrying torches which they were using to fire the arbors.

Brak passed a woman's butchered, armless corpse. Then he saw the body of a young peasant boy similiarly hacked to pieces. Face contorting, he rode on.

The center of the battle seemed to be a confused melee on a rise. There, several dozen unmounted peasants fought a losing struggle against twice as many armed horsemen.

The mist made recognition difficult for Brak as well as for the enemy. But it also gave the barbarian the advantage of surprise. He charged in among the horsemen before they realized he was not one of them.

"Turn back!" he screamed. "Turn back, you child-killing jackals!"

48

From left to right he swung his broadsword in a giant arc. One soldier thrust up his sword to parry. Brak's blade traveled in one side of the man's neck and out the other.

Brak tore his sword loose. A spear raked his ribs. He kicked his pony, thankful for its instant response. Man and horse lunged out of the way in time to avoid a second spear-thrust that would have been fatal.

At the same instant, Brak clamped his left hand on the spear, just below the head. He pulled. The soldier who had aimed at him was jerked forward onto the point of Brak's sword, and gutted.

"Pemma!" Brak hacked back and forth, fending off new attacks. "*Pemma?*"

"Barbarian?" The faint cry came from beyond an arbor all in flames. "This way—"

"Don't bother with yellow-head," screamed a soldier. "The prince is the one we—" Seeing Brak riding at him, sword bared, the soldier hauled back on his pony's reins and tumbled off balance from the saddle.

Brak raced by toward the burning arbor, hewing a path with his great sword. Its edge was thick with dripping blood. Cruel faces floated in from left and right. But few risked direct assault on the huge man who rode like a fury through the drifting plumes of smoke and mist.

All at once, Brak sighted Pemma. The prince had fallen to his knees. He was fighting off three riders who clubbed at him with spear-butts. Brak charged into the attackers, slashing.

His blade sliced under the edge of one man's jerkin, cleaving the man's chest-cage nearly in half. Pemma suddenly saw a way out of the trap. He reached up to grasp Brak's free hand, hoping to be hauled into the saddle.

At that moment Brak half-glimpsed a man on his left and slightly behind. Brak's pony bucked and plunged. The big barbarian sensed that his enemy on the left was driving a sword or spear at his backbone. He tossed his broadsword from right to left hand to fend off the attack.

The strategy failed. The soldier drove the butt of his spear past Brak's upraised arm. The heavy wood caught the big man in the temple and lit weird fires behind his eyes.

"Take the prince!" someone else was shouting. "The

prince is the one that Lady Nordica wants—"

Desperately Brak tried to cut his mounted attacker out of the saddle. His lopping sword-swing missed. Once more the man smashed the spear-butt into the side of Brak's skull.

The barbarian dropped from the saddle, cursing as he fell against the prince and slid past.

Brak struck the earth. All around, hooves stamped wildly, threatening to crush his skull. Pemma yelled. A horse kicked. The point of its hoof struck Brak's forehead. The big man snarled a curse and sprawled unconscious.

Clang-clang-aclang.

The tolling pounded into Brak's skull like the sound of a hammer on an anvil of the gods. Slowly, dizzily, he came awake.

His mouth was full of loam. His body ached. The mist had blown off the fields. An ominous red sundown etched the land in sharp detail: the charred sticks of the arbors; the ruined furrows over which Nordica's men had ridden roughshod; the corpses of the laborers, slaughtered and mutilated.

Brak struggled to his feet. He shook his head to clear it. Then, remembering, he started to run.

"Pemma? Pemma, where are you? Pemma—*answer!*"

The prince was nowhere to be found. In the scarlet sundown the doomsbell in the palace kept tolling.

Chapter IV

ASCENT THROUGH THE MIST

Brak assumed he was still alive only because the attackers must have mistaken him for dead. After searching the furrows for a time, he unearthed his broadsword half-buried in a pile of smoking ash, all that remained of a gutted arbor. One last look at the desolate scene—Nordica's out-riders had methodically slaughtered every last soul toiling in the field, some hundred in all—the big barbarian turned his back on the carnage and trudged toward the palace.

In the palace yard Brak stopped. His face twisted.

Hooftracks showed where the relief force had ridden out. Why, then, hadn't it arrived? He suspected it was be-cause Iskander was not present to lead the soldiers. Doubtless fearing an encounter with Nordica's troops, they had probably gone slinking off in another direction.

Hurrying on through the echoing rooms, Brak found Strann in the audience hall where he had left him. The lord of the kingdom indicated a window embrasure. The dwarf was perched up there.

"The fool saw smoke in the arbors," Strann said. "The—the arbors where my son was working."

Brak nodded dismally. "The witch-woman's riders car-ried him off, Lord."

Strann put his face into his hands. His shoulders shook.

Trying to offer some comfort, Brak added, "But he was alive, I think. All the rest were killed without mercy."

For a moment Brak was afraid the silver-bearded man would collapse. But though Strann's body was wasted, his will was not. He controlled, then subdued, then hid his grief. With his right hand he pushed himself higher, until he was sitting nearly upright. Sundown's light falling through the embrasures painted half his face the color of fresh blood.

"But if my son is not dead," Strann said, "he was taken for a purpose. That is even more terrible."

Brak hunkered down before the dais, frowned. "What purpose could it be? To force you to give up your rule to Nordica, in exchange for his life?"

"Possibly. Or she might want him for one of her occult experiments. There's been much grisly talk that the secrets discovered by Celsus Hyrcanus involved rituals which require—" Strann hesitated "—the sacrifice of human life."

Brak said nothing. A moment later, Strann's shoulders stiffened.

"I will not let her destroy me. Pemma would despise me if I did. There must be some means of learning whether

51

my son is alive or dead and, if alive, why the woman wants him."

As Brak pondered this last, Strann clapped his hands. The dwarf scrambled from the embrasure and ran to the dais. Before the ruler could speak, however, hoofbeats rang in the outer yard.

Brak snorted. "Your troops returning, Lord. Somehow they never reached the vineyards."

Rather than anger, Strann displayed sorrow. He shook his head as if to say he understood why armed fighting men would gallop out and somehow never come to grips with the enemy. When men faced the unknown—even trained fighting men paid to use their weapons—they could not be judged by normal standards of bravery and cowardice. At least that was how Brak read Strann's expression. He did not share the ruler's tolerance.

To the dwarf Strann said, "Ride as fast as you can on donkeyback up to the hills where Ambrose the Pillarite sits. Tell him I bid him search out my son's whereabouts if he can. Also Nordica's plans for him. Return quickly."

The dwarf nodded and hurried away. Curious, Brak asked:

"How can an old man sleeping on top of a rock needle tell you anything?"

"Ambrose the Pillarite has perched up on that shaft since before I was born, Brak. Indeed, no one knows how old he may be. But one thing is certain. He has a mind that is not like ours. He sees over many leagues without stirring from his perch."

"He sees when he sleeps?" Brak shivered.

"Do not ask me to explain how. I cannot. Ambrose is a mystic. He worships some faceless god whose symbol is a peculiar cross, and whose name may never be written. It may be that the Pillarite's power comes from this peculiar god. In any case, he will see Nordica, wherever she is, by whatever means he sends his mind traveling. He will give us word of Pemma."

With a pot of wine in hand, the yellow-haired barbarian settled down on a curule chair, to await the dwarf's return. The longer he stayed in this accursed land, the more bewildered he became.

Of what possible help could an unwashed old anchorite

be in this situation? Brak really didn't put much stock in the Nameless God of the Nestorians. Ambrose's mental powers were probably compounded of one part longevity and one part local superstition.

Yet as Brak waited in silence, he recalled again the peculiar burning strength in his arm, at the moment Elinor the shepherd girl had been about to drop into the Manworm pit.

Had Ambrose the Pillarite given him that strength? Brak could not answer the question.

* * *

An hour passed.

Another.

A servant in shabby livery slipped in to light torches in the cressets and invert the hourglass on its pedestal behind the dais. The darkness increased. The hearth embers burned low. Brak grew sleepy.

He wakened from a doze. The dwarf had come back, covered with dust. He was upon the dais now, whispering into his master's ear.

Strann's expression told the tidings. They were not good.

"What did the Pillarite say?" Brak wanted to know.

"The hermit is sleeping so deeply he could not be wakened."

"Then it's time to put our trust in something besides visions," Brak muttered. "Lord, your son was generous to me this morning. Generous and kind. When I rode to the vineyards, I was not quick enough to save him. So I feel that what happened to him is partly my doing. I feel I should try to bring him back, if that can be done."

"You'd risk your life?"

"When a kindness is done to me, I owe something in return. No matter what it costs."

Strann nodded gravely. "I accept your offer. Take your chair and sleep awhile. Iskander is due back soon. When he arrives, we'll explore our best plan of action."

"You should sleep yourself, Lord."

Eyes somber, Strann said, "With Pemma behind the

walls of Nordica's castle, I cannot."

Twice more the hourglass was turned before Brak again stirred out of his chilly doze, wolf-pelt wrapped around his shoulders. Heavy boots rang on the marble. Iskander strode into the hall, dropped to one knee.

"Lord, we found nary a deserter. The men who ran away are not roaming the countryside. They've all gone over to her."

"Your search was ill timed, through no fault of your own," Strann said. "While you were gone, Pemma was taken by force."

Iskander turned pale. The old man explained in detail, concluding:

"Brak wishes to try to rescue him."

"A fool's notion," Iskander said. Quickly he held up one hand. "Not that I'm against it. Frankly, I'm sick to death of commanding cowards whose bowels turn to water at the mere mention of that red-haired slut. But I suspect the barbarian doesn't understand the situation."

Nettled, Brak said, "Then explain it to me, Captain."

Iskander almost grinned. "Very well. Nordica's castle sits high on the mountain slopes. It's strongly built. Mightily walled. Using the men who have been lured away, she can guard it against siege almost indefinitely. Further, the road up is treacherous. The fog's thick at night, but that's the only feasible time to attack."

Brak ran his thumb down the edge of his broadsword. "What if we attacked not with a hundred men but with one? What if I went up there alone?"

Now, Iskander laughed aloud. To Strann he said, "Lord, we've indeed found a brave man." Strann's nod agreed.

Brak showed his impatience. "Is there any other route up to the castle besides the roadway?"

Iskander shook his head. "None," Iskander said. "The road is the only—" He stopped.

"What are you thinking?" Brak asked.

"Impossibilities."

"Tell me."

"For a moment I was thinking of the sheer cliff on the western side. Just there it forms the lower part of the west

54

castle wall. There are window openings, I think. Unbarred. But you couldn't scale it after dark, in the fog. It's far too treacherous."

"I could try," said Brak in a low voice. "I will, once we learn Pemma's whereabouts."

In hushed tones the three men fell to talking. By the time the night ended and the light through the embrasures grew to a shell-pink hue, they had worked out a rough plan.

Iskander knelt beside the dais. He drew a map of the mountain stronghold by tracing his thumb through hearth-ash sprinkled on the marble. Brak studied the lines symbolizing road, cliffs and castle. Finally he nodded.

"All that remains is to learn whether Pemma lives. And where he is."

Iskander scratched his chin. "Tradesmen call here. Peddlers and such. Perhaps—"

Brak smiled a wolfish smile. "Perhaps we can persuade one of them to help us."

So saying, he hefted his broadsword and stalked out of the hall. Iskander followed in a rush.

* * *

Shortly after sunrise, the palace's main courtyard began to fill with the wagons of bakers and farmers. They were busily unloading supplies for the royal household. Brak squatted next to the wall of the stable. He waited and watched.

Soon a portly potter came in, driving a cart. He began to pull his wares from beneath a blanket. The palace steward bustled out to inform him that there were no funds in the lord's treasury for useless purchases. Then the steward turned his back.

As the potter began to cover his wares again, Brak strode over.

"Good day, peddler." Brak smiled in a way that made the peddler glance up and start. "Uh—good day, sir."

Brak continued to grin. "You'd do better to take your goods up to the castle of the woman they call Nordica Fire-Hair. As a matter of fact, Lord Strann has a mission for you there."

55

The peddler looked horror-struck. "I wouldn't enter those accursed gates for anything! I've heard tales of that woman's evil ways. No, I absolutely would not—sir! What are you doing?"

The barbarian was laying his huge sword across the top of the cart. The sword shone like cold white fire.

"Peddler," Brak breathed, "you will visit Nordica's house after you leave this one, or you'll never leave this one at all."

The peddler's fat belly began to tremble as Brak outlined what was to be done. Brak's expression, plus that blazing sword atop the wagon, soon overcame the tradesman's reluctance. In moments the arrangements were made.

Brak called for servants to unhitch the peddler's quartet of mules. Three would be kept at the palace, together with the cart and most of the pottery. This would assure the man's return.

Brak and Iskander watched the potter set out through the portcullis. He rode bareback on one mule, a few pots in a bag slung over his shoulder. He looked utterly miserable.

Two days crawled by before the peddler rode in again. He sought Strann, Brak and Iskander in the audience hall.

The man looked sallow and perspired much. He appeared to have lost some weight. He said to them in a whining voice:

"As I feared, those in the castle bought nothing."

"But you did get inside?" asked Iskander.

"Aye." The peddler shuddered. "For an hour. That was an hour too much."

"For the sake of your own life," Brak said, "I trust you spent that hour profitably."

The peddler gulped, nodded. "Yes, yes! The prince is alive."

Strann swayed on the couch. "Where—where is he being kept?"

"As nearly as I could learn from the servants with whom I spoke, he's being kept in a cell."

Iskander snorted. "Where else, you infernal simpleton? In what part of the castle is the cell? That's what we need to know!"

56

"The w-w-western part. The cliff side. The lowest row of window openings. I think they told me it was the second window from the left as you looked upward from the road below. I pretended that the prince had done me an injury. I said I wanted to cry obscene oaths at him as I rode away. I thought that was rather clever."

Silence. The peddler's face fell.

"Haven't I done well, masters? I risked my life for you! Now it's only fair that you give me back my goods."

"You may have your goods back with interest," Strann said. "A purse of dinshas for the fellow, Iskander. Make it a fat one."

Soon the peddler was sent on his way with an escort of three mounted riders to see him safely over the border—and to make sure the man did not turn back and betray them to Nordica for extra profit. At nightfall, in a drizzling rain, Brak, Iskander and half-a-dozen grumbling soldiers set out from Strann's palace.

The cold pelted Brak's cheeks as they rode upward through pitch blackness. Presently the rain slacked off, replaced by a clammy, ghostly mist that folded around them.

After an interminable time, Iskander called a soft command. The file of riders halted.

"There, Brak," Iskander whispered, pointing.

High overhead in the murk Brak saw faint smears of orange.

"Torches on the battlements?" he asked.

"Yes."

The barbarian climbed down from his pony. Although the night was cold, and made colder by the fog, he unfastened the wolf-pelt, cast it aside. He strode to the base of the cliff. It seemed unbelievably high and sheer. He ran his palm over the rock.

"Wet. Bad for footholds."

"It'll be no better any other night," Iskander told him. "The fog is almost constant here."

"Then give me the coil."

One of the soldiers handed down a great loop of heavy rope. Brak wound it round and round about his right shoulder. Broadsword bumping his left thigh, he pulled

57

himself up to the first low escarpment and looked back down.

Iskander and his mounted soldiers were wraiths in the dark. "Pemma will come down first if I find him," Brak called.

"Understood," Iskander called in return. "The gods be with you."

With only a low grumble for a reply, Brak reached upward.

He felt for a handhold, pulled himself up to a ledge, sniffed.

The face of the cliff was not as sheer as it appeared from below. It was quite rough and had an ample number of places for grasping. But the fog, blown on a wind that seemed stronger up here, had coated the outcrops with slimy dampness. Cautiously Brak began climbing again.

He had gone perhaps five times his own height when his foot slipped.

Both his legs slid from under him. Desperately his fingers scrabbled for a purchase. He kicked his right knee forrward, felt it strike a narrow ledge. Pain blazed through his body. His left leg slid off into space.

With a strangled curse he held onto the rocks he was gripping and slowly, slowly raised his left leg up until he again stood on the ledge.

Above, the torches burned brighter. Below, only the fog whirled. Iskander and his riders had vanished, as had the land itself. Brak leaned his cheek against the cliff and gulped.

The broadsword hanging at his hip made climbing awkward. His fingers were already laced with cuts and gashes from the sharp rock. The heavy rope coil weighted his right shoulder like a stone. For a moment he was overwhelmed with a feeling of being lost between the earth and the sky in a limbo of nothingness.

After resting a moment longer on the ledge from which he'd nearly slipped to his death, Brak reached high and began to climb again.

The wind grew louder. It sounded like a forlorn, abandoned soul wailing in pain. Overhead Brak began to make out the blurred silhouette of the castle battlements.

Suddenly the rope coil slipped from his shoulder.

Instinctively Brak whipped his left hand across to catch it. He swayed, arched backwards, a moment away from falling—

Wildly he flung his left hand back to the cliff. He grasped a knob of rock, held on while his right hand twisted around to push the rope coil into position again.

His huge chest ached with exertion. The dampness of the fog mixed with his own sweat on his skin. He hung backwards, away from the cliff face. Only his left hand gripping the rock kept him from tumbling into the abyss.

Tightening the muscles of that left arm, Brak slowly pulled himself inward. Finally he leaned against the cliff.

A night bird went flapping by. Brak swallowed hard, began climbing—

As he neared the place where the cliff became the foundation of the castle wall, his foot came down hard on a protruding rock. It crumbled the moment he put weight on it.

Bits of rock sheared away, went clattering down into the emptiness, making a great racket.

Brak crouched against the cliff. He heard voices overhead, calling to one another. He risked a glance toward the battlement, saw helmeted heads outlined in flickering torchlight.

Brak held his breath. His whole body ached as he clung there on the edge of that awful emptiness.

Finally the guards disappeared.

Brak clambered upward again. He reached high for the sill of the second black opening in the lower row of windows.

His legs hung free as he clung to the stone sill with both hands. He dragged himself upward using his arms alone. This was the critical moment.

There was silence inside the cell. Brak knew he didn't dare startle Pemma or his guards. Yet there would be noise, and no avoiding it. He tensed—

He pulled up hard, flung his left leg over the sill. His broadsword clanked as he went through the window and struck the floor, tumbling.

Before he stopped rolling, someone cried out.

Lashing out with his right hand, Brak encountered flesh, clamped his fingers over Pemma's mouth. The prince was struggling to sit up on a rude stone sleeping bench.

"No sound!" Brak whispered. "None, or we'll never get out! It's Brak. I have a rope."

Slowly Pemma's thrashings subsided. Brak let him go. Through a small grille in the door, distant lamplight gleamed. Pemma's ruddy face shone with sweat.

Brak located a thrust-out stone in one wall, began lashing the end of the rope around it.

When he had tied the rope securely, he pushed Pemma toward the window.

"Go out and down. And hurry."

Pemma didn't waste time questioning his deliverer. He crawled over the sill, grasped the rope and slipped into the fog.

Breathing hard, Brak waited. He kept one hand on the rope to check its tension. A footfall in the corridor startled him. He swung around. The broadsword scabbard hit the stone sleeping bench with a clang.

The guard's head appeared beyond the door grille.

"Prisoner? What's all the racket? Answer me!"

Abruptly Brak felt the tension leave the rope. Pemma had reached the ground quickly. Brak's choice loomed cruel and clear: if he fled now, arousing the guard's suspicion, he might set the stage for discovery of the rescue party on the road below. But if he stayed—

The guard was already fitting a key into the rusty lock. "Prisoner? Speak up in there!"

"Nothing wrong." Brak kept his voice down to a nearly inaudible growl. "I cried out in a nightmare, that's all."

Even as Brak spoke, the guard was replying:

"Perhaps I'd better see what you're up to—"

The key racketed in ancient iron.

Cursing his ill luck, Brak tore the rope loose from its anchoring-place. He hurled the loose end through the open window just as the door started to squeal open.

Brak flung himself full length on the stone bench. He pulled up a flimsy coverlet and lay curled on his left side, his back to the door as it opened full. He hoped his body and the coverlet would conceal his broadsword.

"Let me sleep," he mumbled. "Go away and let me sleep."

The guard remained in the doorway. He peered at the dim form on the bench, grunted.

"Well, everything seems in order. But no more yelling. I want to get some rest myself."

Ponderously the door clanged shut.

Brak lay on his side a long time, staring at the blackness of the wall.

Pemma had been freed. But the price was high.

At dawnlight, with shouting and cursing, the guards discovered him and hauled him down through musty passages to Nordica Fire-Hair.

Chapter V

WITCHLAIR

Strangely, Brak found himself able to laugh inwardly at his ironic predicament.

Three guards manhandled him through a series of rock-walled corridors. They brought him to a high, dim chamber whose few windows were covered with thin slivers of jade leaded together, forming panes. Light from the sky turned a deep underwater emerald inside that room.

Brak was shoved down three marble steps. He noticed several globes of golden wire, a gilt starglass and other items of occult paraphernalia strewn on taborets and low benches. In one corner, more than a hundred rolled-up parchments were piled. His inner laughter died for a moment, replaced by wonder. He had never imagined that that many separate books existed in the world.

The largest guard, a suet-faced fellow with a twisting white scar on his jawline, said, "Hold him tightly while I waken the lady."

The man crossed the chamber and passed behind a hanging. A small bell chimed. This time Brak laughed.

"Stop that!" said one of the remaining guards. "You'll make her all the more angry."

In response Brak threw back his head and let his mirth bellow out.

It was a release, that gargantuan laughter that rang in the eerie green-lit hall. His predicament was more than a little desperate, and he was well aware of it. But he'd never been one to dwell overlong on private dread, preferring instead, when he could, to make a mockery of danger and thereby unman it. His laughter was a deliberate tactic, and one which had the desired effect:

"I said stop it!" the guard exclaimed, giving Brak's arm a shake.

"Let me go and I will," Brak roared between gusts of laughter.

"Mad," the other guard whispered. "Possessed."

"A berserker?" responded the first. "He has the look in his eyes, right enough—"

"You simpletons, release me!" Brak thundered. "I'm not going to run, nor even fight! Else—" A huge swallow of air; another mighty laugh. "—else why would I have let you take my sword away, eh?"

"A point, there," speculated the second guard.

"'Ware!" the first responded. "You said there was some devil in his mind and I believe it!"

"Wrong," Brak gasped. "I'm just seeing things the right way round. I marked your faces when you walked into that cell and discovered who I really was. You were bleached white. 'Tis the first trick anyone's taken from your lady since I rode into this cursed land. I find that amusing, don't you? Very amus—"

The laughter died in his throat, drowned by a sound from behind the hanging.

The sound was a wail of exquisite pain.

Next a woman's voice:

"—down a rope? Down a *rope,* you incredible imbeciles?"

And the large guard appeared, tottering, his right cheek ripped open by a long cut that oozed blood.

Nordica followed him into the chamber. She carried a

dagger with a half-moon blade. She trembled visibly. Her copper hair shimmered in the greenish light as she advanced on the bleeding guard:

"Take yourself out of my sight before I rip your belly open for good measure."

The guard scuttled backwards as Nordica swept past him. Her white silk robe belled around her bare feet. Brak's amusement was dwindling rapidly, the glitter in the girl's eyes was the shine of unadulterated venom.

Nordica's jade eyes fixed on Brak. "Guffaw while you can, barbarian," she said. "I warned you to ride on. You'll regret you didn't."

Brak met that unsettling gaze, forced a chuckle. "But you've lost this part of the game, witch-woman."

Nordica seethed. "You soldiers—leave me alone with him. Two of you remain outside the door. One of you speak to my commander. Get the men working. By sundown I want every last opening in the western wall sealed with stone and mortar. Go!"

As the guards wheeled and hurried out, Brak had an impulse to seize Nordica by her slender white throat and choke her. Perhaps he could kill her before the guards reached him. But he hesitated. Not from fear. Out of a desire to learn something of what she plotted, here in this green-lit room. Something that might help Strann and Prince Pemma win against her. Provided, of course, that he could stay alive to tell them about it.

Crossing her arms, Nordica paced back and forth in front of Brak. "You came up the cliff?"

"Yes."

"No one has ever climbed that cliff before. No one."

"Two have now. I climbed up. Pemma climbed down."

"You got the bad end of the bargain. You'll die for it."

"That may be so," Brak said. "Still, you wanted the prince. You no longer have him. So I can laugh a little at your expense."

A curious silence settled on the chamber. Nordica inclined her head. She studied Brak's huge chest, his muscled legs below the lion-hide at his waist. Two spots of angry color faded from her cheeks. A smile curled the corners of her mouth.

All at once Brak found that his desire to laugh had

64

passed. His backbone crawled as the girl's jade eyes slowly moved from one part of his body to the next, as though he were some sort of joint or hock being scrutinized for its potential on the spit.

The emerald gloom seemed to deepen. Nordica's eyes seemed to glow the more brightly, tiny whorls and specks of light turning within their depths. Once again Brak was gripped by the awful, unclean feeling he'd experienced at the caravansary.

This woman was utter evil.

And far worse—she was evil he should recognize.

"Perhaps," Nordica said at length, "I can think of a better fate for you than simple death. Prince Pemma's escape might be good fortune, not ill."

"Say what you mean, woman."

Nordica walked slowly to a low pile of silken cushions. She sat down, clasping her arms around her knees. She gazed at him with those eyes that seemed to mask a private amusement. Her scent drifted heavy, musky, oppressive with the suggestion of something putrefied hidden within its very sweetness.

Her voice became almost gay. "I mean, outlander, that perhaps you may serve me as well as the prince. That is to say—" A tinkling laugh. "Your carcass may."

"For what purpose do you need bodies, woman? More of your magic?"

"How clever of you! Of course. Something remarkable is about to happen in this crude and provincial corner of the world. When it is accomplished—well, you'll see some equally remarkable changes in every kingdom between the steppes and Khurdisan."

She hesitated, almost as if expecting the name to be of significance to him. Brak kept his face immobile. Yet again some instinct told him that this creature knew far more of him than he suspected.

"What's your remarkable happening to be, woman?"

"Something my departed father was too squeamish to bring about."

"The alchemical secret?"

Nordica's laugh was cruelly chiding. "You've been listening to the tales of the clods in the field."

"And most interesting tales they are," he returned.

"About a model daughter who one day became something quite different."

At this Nordica showed her contempt. "I am no different than I have always been. I am the daughter of Celsus Hyrcanus."

"Some say otherwise."

Starting away, she spun back. "What?"

"Some say the change was so abrupt, you might be another woman entirely."

"That shows how much those filthy peasants know!"

Nordica turned her back to him, but not before he glimpsed a curious opacity in her jade eyes, as though she had masked and hid the secrets with which she'd been silently taunting him.

"For years," she continued over her shoulder, "I loathed my father's scrupulous prattle about using his powers to respectable ends. Respectable! What a vile, hypocritical word. There is no respectability in this world except false respectability. Evil is the nature of man. Of the world!"

Rather stolidly, Brak replied, "I have no fixed opinion on that."

"Then you're a fool as my father Celsus was. He found the secret but refused to use it."

"He offered it to Lord Strann, I understand."

"That's throwing it away!"

"Then how would you use it, woman?"

Like a hiss: "To conquer!"

"Conquer what?"

She dismissed the question. "In good time, barbarian. In good time."

Brak snorted. "Say no more. I understand you too well."

"You don't understand that I am and always have been the daughter of Celsus."

"Must we debate the point? It hardly seems important."

"You apparently have some notion that I'm not what I seem. You brought the matter up."

"My error." Then he lied. "I have no interest in who you are."

"Ah." The weird, coruscating lights returned to her eyes. She was mocking again. "I thought perhaps you sensed something—familiar in me."

"That's true," he growled. "I've seen evil before."

It didn't anger her. Rather, she seemed pleased. "Well, as for those ridiculous prattlings about my supposed change in behavior, I can only tell you that I was dissembling up until the time that my father—ah"—a supple gesture—"met with an untimely fate. I knew many years ago that if my father did happen onto the alchemical secret, he would never take advantage of its true worth. I pretended to be the most modest of maidens, the most dutiful of daughters, so that he would continue his work, never suspecting that I coveted—his secrets"—a quick, almost involuntary fisting of one slim hand—"for larger gains."

By this time Nordica had walked away from Brak, gliding to a part of the chamber where shadows clotted together and the gloom made reading her eyes difficult. That, in a way, was a blessing.

He decided that she protested too much. She had described her relationship with her father in the style of one who had committed a story to memory. He was sure she was not telling the entire truth.

He was even more sure when she glided from the shadows to confront him again. Her eyes danced with those jeweled green lights that spoke a hellish language of their own:

Beware my words, barbarian, those eyes seemed to say. *Beware my secrets which you can only guess.*

If she was maintaining the fiction that she had always behaved this way—privately both craving her father's knowledge and despising his principles—she must really be doing so not for his benefit but for someone else's.

For those who dwelled nearby? The farmers? The courtiers? He didn't know. But she had repeated her explanation as though it were expected of her. At the same time her eyes told him something entirely different, almost daring him to discover what she might be.

Brak's temples began to ache from the tormenting maze of this game.

Perhaps tiredness and the strain of capture were making him imagine all of it. At any rate, if Nordica indeed owned the secret which savants and wizards had been

67

hunting since time forgot, well might she make her quiet promise of conquest come true.

But conquest of what? This kingdom? Kingdoms beyond? She had referred to the entire world. He pondered it a moment.

With the alchemical secret as source of her power, Nordica might indeed truly devastate the world from land's end to land's end. Men would flock to her as they were already doing in Strann's kingdom. There would be cataclysmic wars. The big barbarian had a bleak, fitful vision of armies marching, cities burning, the sky boiling with black clouds and with fire while the dying screamed from ditches and burial-pits. And Nordica Fire-Hair rode in her chariot with Scarletjaw beside her and a sphere of solid gold in one upraised hand—

He shook himself out of the devastating reverie. Better to be practical. To discover just whether the keystone of all her threats really existed:

"Answer me one thing, woman."

"What?"

"Do you really know how to transmute lead into gold? Or is that only more dissembling?"

"Haven't I said I know the secret?"

"How did you get it from your father?"

"That is my affair."

"Still more secrets, eh? Maybe it's all one huge lie." And his smile was barbarously taunting.

Nordica's eyes sparked with anger. Brak's taunt sent her striding back and forth across the marble floor as decisively as any man:

"Transmutation is not a myth but a truth. It requires a ritual—one which will prove to you that the secret is indeed mine."

Now his spine tickled with fear again. "How so?"

"Part of that ritual demands the presence of four human beings. Each represents one of the four elements of creation—earth, air, fire, and water." She paused. "Doesn't that tell you why Pemma was brought here while the rest of his workers were left behind?"

"Left behind dead and butchered," Brak echoed flatly. "Pemma was to be one of the four?"

"The earth," Nordica said. "He is no warrior, though

68

he comes of king's blood. He has a greater affinity for the land. At heart he's a peasant."

"And with four—captives—you can perform the ritual?"

"Yes. It is the secret my father spent a lifetime to unearth."

"How many others have fallen into your trap? How many sets of four have you slaughtered trying this hell-ritual?"

"None, barbarian. You and the other three sacrifices who are even now chained in a cell are the first four. Pemma, by the way, should have been likewise chained the moment my men fetched him here. However, I wanted to talk with him first. You arrived before I had a chance to break away from my studies and summon him."

"Witch-woman," Brak said, taking a step toward her, "you used a word I don't like. Sacrifices."

Nordica darted behind a low taboret inlaid with chips of pearl. "Keep your distance. Else I'll call those guards outside and you'll have a spear in your spine. Be civil to me, Brak. I can help make the end of your life much less painful."

A thick muscle in Brak's neck bunched. His mouth twisted. "Sacrifices. Blood-killings. Abominations!"

But Nordica only smiled. "Perhaps so, barbarian, but they will be successful ones. I'm impatient to begin. Soon I will."

Gracefully she walked to one of the jade windows.

"Out there, Brak, the winds blow seasonally strong. In a few days they will rise. The winds must be summoned before the ritual of transmutation can be worked. The four winds, Brak. From the four corners of the earth. Combined with the four elements, they will accomplish the transmutation. I know how to summon the winds. And when I do—turning base metal to gold—there'll be no end to my power."

In the grim silence she studied him. Then:

"I think I was in error to complain about losing Pemma. You may not be a farmer like Pemma the Prince. But you're a man of the earth in your own way. Strong. With the earth's strength in your arms. Yes, I think you'll do excellently in Pemma's place when the four winds rise."

Brak scowled. "Before I let myself be dragged into your scheme, I'll kill every man who comes near me. And myself in the bargain."

"Dear me! So ferocious. What's happened to your laughter?"

"Gone. I'm sorry. I let them drag me from the cell where they found me. Better I had died there then lend even small help to your plans."

Briefly fury blazed bright in the witch-girl's eyes. Then, controlling it, she walked around to where Brak stood with his powerful legs planted wide apart, his hands doubled, red anger making his broad shoulders quake.

"Brak, Brak—" Her voice was musical, full of Lorlei-notes. "Why struggle so?"

"What do you expect, witch-woman? Praise for what you intend to do?"

"At least you could make your stay with me tolerable, even if the ending is foreordained."

Again Nordica touched his arm. She tightened her sweetly-perfumed fingers. Her nails dug his flesh.

"Did I not tell you, Brak, that night at the caravansary, how much I admire a courageous man? Even though your courage is worthless now, it's still a commodity to be desired. I need your strength when the winds rise. And you'll die. But you can take pleasure with me in the meantime."

Brak's mind reeled and blackened. For a swift, blurred instant, he saw not the face and jade eyes of Nordica, but the incredibly dark hair, the pale skin, the seething eyes of Ariane.

Ariane the offspring of Septegundus. The Nestorians called her Daughter of Hell.

He remembered how she had taken him up into the sky in a fabulous chariot. Or was that only illusion?

In either case, she had showed him visions: the kingdoms of the world spread beneath him, including, far southward, sunlit Khurdisan.

Ariane's mouth had been full of soft, seductive words. She promised him all he saw on that enchanted flight if he would but love her. And she promised him delights sufficient to madden even the most jaded voluptuary. Her beauty was such that he had been tempted to say yes.

70

Her price—her only price—was his acceptance of Yob-Haggoth as his master and the keeper of his soul. So he defied her and spat at the idea.

No doubt she'd died hating him, there in the thundering chaos at the ruined shrine in the Ice-marches. But it all came back to him in sights and sounds and gut-wrenching memories as he stared at Nordica Fire-Hair and saw, shimmering and shifting somewhere behind her face, a second face.

Ariane's.

Brak twisted away from Nordica, disgusted by her glib way of condemning him to death one instant and making crude advances the next. His forehead ran with sweat. His huge chest shone with it. He breathed hard, sensing that he had come quite close to some awful hint of the truth that was struggling to escape from the depths of his mind—

What rubbish! Brought on by the tensions of the moment, nothing more. The resemblance between the overtures made by Ariane and Nordica was superficial coincidence.

Wasn't it?

*   *   *

Nordica seemed momentarily uncertain of her next move. While she hesitated, Brak decided that he'd already waited too long to take positive action.

He let his glance slide round the chamber, seeking some object he might use as a weapon. He could no longer endure this red-haired witch-woman. He could no longer endure being treated like an animal on a chain, a human Scarletjaw who performed tricks whose meaning eluded him while they brought Nordica vile amusement.

She gave him no chance to pursue his search. She thrust against him, hair warm on his cheek. It smelled of that sweetish, rotting scent.

"Is my suggestion really so revolting, Brak? Am I ugly?"

"Outwardly? No. But deep inside—inside you are—"

The word ready on Brak's tongue was a vulgar

71

marketplace term. He never uttered it. The girl's cheeks darkened. Anger lit her eyes again and she backed away.

"I'm the mistress here! I will not tolerate this!"

Mystified by her behavior, Brak prepared to strike back if she came at him with a hidden blade. Instead, he was startled when she rushed by him. She ran to an ornamental lattice which decorated one area of the chamber wall.

She gave the interlaced pattern of carved wood a close scrutiny. Then she hurried on, up the chamber steps. In a moment she was outside.

"Guards! This way! Swords ready."

Brak was alone. And utterly baffled.

Somewhere in the rock-walled corridors outside, Nordica's soldiers yelled. So did another man. He sounded frightened. Brak raced for the stairs. This might be his chance to escape—

Half way to the steps he hauled up short. The guards crowded back into the doorway, thrusting a struggling, spluttering man ahead of them.

A section of the man's robe tore. A guard was left standing holding a scrap of ebony cloth decorated with silver threads.

The man was Tamar Zed.

Nordica appeared behind the soldiers. She stalked round the red-cheeked Magian. Tamar waved at the soldiers.

"These unspeakable dogs laid hands on me!"

"By my order!" Nordica retorted. "When I showed you the spy hole in the lattice, Magian, it was so that we might watch my father here in his workroom."

The Magian flushed even more deeply. Nordica approached Brak, pointed to the lattice.

"Do you see it, barbarian? The third interstice in the fifth row. The hole leads to a small room adjoining. I thought I caught a glimpse of white a moment ago, as though a cheek were pressed tight against the hole. I was right."

Brak saw the break in the lattice pattern, now that it had been pointed out. The Magian straightened his torn robe and threw his shoulders back, looking more arrogant by the moment.

"He was watching us?" Brak asked.

Nordica nodded. "His jealousy wearies me."

"I was a fool to believe everything you told me," Tamar exclaimed.

"Especially when I told you that your caress delighted me, Tamar?" Again Nordica laughed. She walked over to the Magian, touched his cheek. "Once perhaps it did. But it does no longer." Without warning she dug her nails into his flesh. When he cried out, she laughed and darted away. There was fresh blood on the Magian's cheek.

"Exactly why were you watching me, Tamar?" Nordica demanded.

Tamar's dark brows pulled together. He fingered his bloodied cheek.

"Will you shame me in front of him, Nordica?" he muttered. "Don't do it. I warn you. Don't disgrace me this way."

"Who disgraced you in the first place, you jealous imbecile? You disgraced yourself!"

So shaken was Tamar, he could barely gesture at Brak. "That you'd simper and posture in front of this—this *clod*, this *peasant* with his dull stare—is unbelievable."

"He's more of a man than you'll be in ten lifetimes."

The witch-girl had gone too far. Tamar took two swift steps forward. Nordica signaled.

The spears of the guards flashed up, ready to be thrown. Tamar sensed the motion from the corner of a eye, hesitated. But his obviously twisted passion for the girl forced words from his lips:

"To treat me this way when you know how I feel about you—!"

Tamar stopped. He eyed the glittering spearheads. He kept his embittered silence.

"What do you suggest I do with the outlander?" Nordica asked, tormenting him.

"Kill him," Tamar said. "Feed him to Scarletjaw."

"And what if I refuse? What will you do then? Take yourself out of my house? I doubt it, Magian. For a great many reasons, I doubt it. It is my mind, mine alone, holding the secret. The final phrases needed to make the ritual work, to make the four winds rise, to make the life-stuff drain from the captives. And remember the delights I can

74

offer, Magian. Provided I am not so angry that I withhold them."

For a long moment Tamar Zed glared at Nordica, plainly hating her and loving her at the same time. Finally, in a shuddering voice, he whispered:

"You know me far too well. You know I can't turn away from this place, or you."

This time Nordica's laugh was genuine, delighted.

"Leave me, Tamar. Never again let me discover you spying on me, or the foolish people in this land will have another death to whisper about besides that of Celsus Hyrcanus."

Gathering his robe around him, Tamar Zed departed. Trying to maintain his dignity by his arrogant posture, he walked up the stairway. Only once did he turn, to stare at Brak. What his black eyes promised the barbarian was nothing short of death.

After the Magian had gone, Nordica dismissed her guards. When the doors swung shut, she indicated the cushions in the center of the floor.

"Sit with me a while longer, Brak. Drink a goblet of wine."

"I see no reason for that."

She reached out to touch his face. His belly tightened, because he half expected that she'd dig her nails into his flesh as she'd done with Tamar Zed. Instead, she stroked his face with the gentlest of touches. Her eyes seemed to enlarge to green moons, their oblique secret thrusting to the fore once more.

Brak's mind dulled. He saw great churning lights within those eyes. A wind keened in his ears, over which he heard her say:

"Treat me kindly, barbarian."

Kindly! When she meant to slaughter him? He wanted to roar.

Somehow he couldn't. The power of those luminous eyes held him wordless as she crooned on:

"Aye, kindly. You have powerful appetites. So it is with me. You may think I am a woman beyond your experience but I am not. We are not strangers, Brak. Don't you recognize that? Can't you tell? *We are not strangers—*"

75

Revulsion helped fight off the dreadful lassitude and dizziness that her voice and eyes conjured. She brought her mouth close. Her lips shone.

"Is my suggestion of a moment ago so unwelcome, Brak? *Stay with me—*"

"No, lady," he said in a strangled voice. "Let the Magian rut after you. I will not. You're a used thing."

She struck him twice in the face.

Brak's head snapped back from the surprising power of the blows. His mind cleared.

"Be careful!" she breathed. "I can make you wish you'd never seen the light of this world. I have offered you pleasure, an interlude of love and—"

"Lady," Brak broke in calmly. "I would sooner plant a kiss on a corpse."

Nordica turned pale. "Then you shall! See how you prefer the dungeon where the other three sacrifices are chained. See how you prefer being fettered with them in the dark."

And, with her robes trailing out behind, she hurried up the stairs and flung wide the doors.

"Soldiers? Take him. The peasant stink of him sickens me. Put him with the other three, below."

The guards swarmed around Brak, pinning his arms. They pushed him up the staircase. As they turned out into the corridor, Brak had a last glimpse of Nordica Fire-Hair alone in the center of the dim, greenish room. Her eyes glowed large and strange and angry.

Despite the ring of steel around him, the curses and cuffs of his captors, Brak was glad to be free of the woman's presence.

As he stumbled along, he tried to grasp the significance of what had just transpired. His mind rang with her peculiar words. *We are not strangers.* A thought that was horror crawled into his consciousness.

Where the thought came from he had no way of telling. Perhaps from his weariness. Perhaps from the coincidental way his route into this cursed land had been guided— predestined, almost—by the mysterious rockslide. Suddenly he found himself asking himself terrible questions.

Had the daughter of Septegundus perished in the Ice-marches after all?

Had Ariane of Hell died with her father's enchanted dagger buried in her back?

Septegundus had said *I will be there*—

Stop it! Nordica was Nordica, no one else.

Wasn't she?

Lunacy, he decided. He'd thought of Ariane only because of the similar way he had rejected both the women, putting down their appeals to the most lascivious side of his nature. For an aching moment he remembered Queen Rhea of Phrix. How easy it would have been to have stayed with her and spared himself these travails—

Enough! he said to himself. It was time for concern about what would happen to him next.

The guards led him onward through the dank, badly-lit corridors. At one point they emerged onto a short rampart running between two round turrets. Brak reveled in the feel of the mist damp against his face.

A clang of armor, shouting, a ferocious snarling drifted from below. The guards halted. One ran to the parapet, peered over.

"The prince!" he exclaimed with a grin. "And a party of men. Come to rescue this brute, I'll wager. The lady has already loosed Scarletjaw on them."

Brak lunged for the rampart's edge.

Hands clawed at his back. Spear butts pounded at his skull. He hung onto the parapet, staring down for one distorted moment upon a scene of horror on the roadway leading up to the castle.

The great hound with its dull iron-gray hide leaped and plunged among Pemma's dozen fighting men. Broadswords snapped against the hard hide. Men and horses dropped, chewed in half, their blood bubbling out.

A spear crashed behind Brak's ear. The edges of the scene below grew dark. He roared Pemma's name but the prince didn't hear. Watching the last of his men perish, Pemma whirled his horse around and thundered down the road.

Scarletjaw loped after him.

The dog turned back after a short distance. Its tongue lolled, spilling blood-drops on the ground. Brak knew

77

there was no hope for him now. Perhaps there never had been.

With a wild scream he spun around, determined to sell his life dearly. He charged the soldiers.

Half-a-dozen spear butts slammed against his skull. Brak toppled over on his face. Despair claimed him the moment before the inside of his brain turned black.

Chapter VI

EARTH, AIR, FIRE, WATER

When Brak opened his eyes, he thought that time had somehow slipped.

He thought he had returned across the intervening days to the Manworm's lair. Close above him he saw an oval face, softly sculptured. As he struggled up, he felt weights on his wrists. Chains clanked. The back of his skull ached.

He heard whisperings. The girl's face seemed to float closer in the poor light. Then it slowly lost its blurred quality.

The girl turned away, spoke to the dark:

"He's wakened. It's the stranger I told you about. The one who helped me. Called Brak."

"See whether he has any clever notions about helping us," replied a reedy male voice.

"Where—" Brak stumbled to his feet, blinking. "Where is this place? Another cell?"

"Aye," said still a third voice. It was rougher than the others, a bass rumbling. "Far down inside the witch-woman's keep. If I'd hid instead of standing my ground when the riders swooped down on my forge, I wouldn't be penned here with the rest of you swine, either."

The reedy voice exclaimed, "It's our predicament together, Runga. Let's not quarrel."

"I'll look after myself, one-leg," Runga answered. "You do the same."

Now Brak managed to make out details of the dungeon. It was a large, vaulted place with straw littering the floor. Voices bounced off the walls, a weird, subterranean sound. The only illumination was the lamplight filtering through a barred aperture in a door.

By this weak gleam Brak could study the face of the shepherd girl kneeling by him.

"Elinor," he said. "How did you come here?"

"I might ask you the same. Two soldiers who serve Nordica set on me, on the slopes above the Manworm's den. It happened the very day I met you. I've been here since, shackled up and not knowing what's to become of me, or these men either."

And Elinor lifted her right wrist to display a thick iron cuff.

The links from the cuff ran to a similar one on Brak's left forearm. Midway along this piece of chain, another chain ran to a ring imbedded in the slimy stone of the wall.

The two other occupants of the cell approached. Runga was burly, thick-chested, powerful-looking. The other man was old, spindly, had a wooden shaft in place of his left leg. The men were chained together in the same fashion as Brak and Elinor.

"What's to become of us?" Brak repeated. "That I can tell you, Elinor—but wait a moment."

He swung toward Elinor. "After you ran away from me at the Manworm cave, I thought I sensed someone watching, from behind the rocks. It must have been Nordica's soldiers."

"It must have been," she agreed.

Brak touched her hand gently. "As near as I can tell from what Nordica has said, you were brought here that day because you live on the high mountain slopes. Because you can symbolize the element air in the ritual she plans to conduct. I was taken in Prince Pemma's place to represent the earth. You there——" He indicated Runga, whose coarse face looked unfriendly. "Did I hear you mention forges? Are you a smith?"

79

Runga nodded. "The best hereabouts, until that devil-woman carried me off."

"She must have chosen you because you're closely associated with fire. While you, stranger——"

"Darios is my name," piped the one-legged man, who wore a circlet of gold through his pierced right ear. "I don't know what you're talking about. Fully, anyway. But I see my part in it. I am—or was—the mate on a trading galley which sailed out of the Port-of-Knives. A fortnight ago, I left the seacoast to return inland because my brother had died. After the burial rites, I started back to port. I was passing through this country when a band of soldiers set on me at the inn where I'd stopped the night. Now I have a question. Plainly we've stumbled into the lair of some madwoman. Each of us represents one of the elements of creation, mine being water, I suppose. But what's the reason for it all?"

In simple terms, Brak explained a little of Nordica's past—at least as it was publicly discussed; he kept his personal suspicions to himself. He described the nature of the ritual as best he knew it—four human sacrifices, each representing a basic substance of the world. He concluded:

"Evidently, for the ritual to succeed, the witch-woman must wait till the seasonal winds rise. She maintains that she can then summon the four great winds from the corners of the earth. That is when our time will come."

"Mercy!" the sailor Darios screeched. "Mercy, gods! To think that I should ever meet such a fate!"

With an ugly growl Runga reached over and cuffed the weaker man. "Be quiet with that sniveling! I don't like this predicament any better than you. But caterwauling won't help."

"Nor will hurting someone smaller than yourself," Brak said quietly. "We're together in this, as the sailor said."

Runga's thick lips twisted. "Are we? Has someone appointed you our leader, to make official pronouncements?"

Anger bubbled up in the big barbarian. He fought it, stifled a retort. Elinor had begun to cry softly. Tears traced silver paths down her cheeks. Brak put his hand across the shoulder of her woolen gown. At his touch she quieted a little.

"There has to be a way of escape," Brak said to them, not fully believing it. "We'll find it. We have time before she needs us as sacrifices."

Elinor shuddered against his chest, frail, terrified. "There isn't any way."

"Frankly," the smith Runga put in, squatting down in a corner like some oversized simian, "I wouldn't mind surrendering my life to that red-haired wench if she'd give me a favor or two. In fact there's not much I wouldn't do to have a woman like that, even for an hour. And in case the rest of you think I'm being disloyal, you're perfectly right."

Darios tugged at his pierced ear. To Brak he said, "The woman has tempted our friend sorely. He's talked of nothing else but her since first they penned him in here."

A growl of contempt rumbled in Brak's throat. "Then you have little notion of the rot inside her mind, blacksmith."

Runga spat on the straw floor. "I'll take the outside and worry about the rest later. My affairs are mine, no one else's."

Accumulated weariness and frustration overwhelmed Brak then. He lunged to his feet, the wrist chain clanking.

"Speak out plainer, smith. There are four of us tied together in this rock room, with the same fate in store for all. I will not wait and do nothing until the time comes for Nordica to kill us. Nor, I think, will this girl or our sailor friend. But what about you? Do you stand with us or not?"

A sneer wrenched Runga's face. "I stand on my own, outlander. I'll do what I wish, when I wish. And if that red-haired creature crooks a finger and bids me come to her, why, perhaps I'll go. If the rest of you don't like it, to the pit with you! Now does that make it plain enough? Even a half-naked savage should understand—"

With a low yell Brak jumped across the cell, jerked up short by the chain. But still he managed to fasten his hands on Runga's throat:

"You'd sell yourself to that witch-slut and let the rest of us die—?"

81

Coughing, choking, the smith flailed at Brak's huge, constricting hands. And abruptly Brak realized that anger had driven him to a cruel, purposeless act. He released his grip.

But Runga had been goaded. He struck back.

His bent knee caught Brak in the midsection, hard. The barbarian gasped. Quickly Runga formed a loop from his chain, and tried to whip it around Brak's throat.

Yellow braid flying, Brak backed off. He half-crouched, ready for the fight he himself had provoked.

"Very well," Runga rumbled. "Let's see who rules our little cell kingdom."

The seaman Darios tottered between them. "Stop it, both of you! This gains us nothing!"

Elinor dragged at Brak's arm. He pushed her away. "I'll give this lout what he deserves."

"Haven't you any thought for the rest of us?" Elinor cried. "A moment ago you said we couldn't escape from this place unless we worked together. I believed you! Now you intend to make certain we can't escape. We'll only defeat or own chances by spilling each other's blood—"

Runga chuckled. "I'd enjoy watching his blood run out. It's probably yellow-colored, like his spine."

Brak took a step, ready for killing. But the pleas of the shepherd girl and Darios finally penetrated his rage-reddened mind. With a disgusted snarl he dropped the length of chain he'd meant to use as a weapon. It struck the floor with a heavy clank.

Brak wiped a forearm across his brow. He said:

"You're right. We need every hand, every set of brains, weak though they may be."

The barb amused Runga. "You refer to yours, eh, barbarian?" And he turned his back and swaggered off to a corner of the cell. His chuckling said he was convinced that he'd carried the day.

Brak stared after the smith. He was disgusted with himself for allowing the bully to override him. Yet he knew he would soon become responsible for the other two prisoners. He was stronger than they were, plainly more accustomed to fighting. And what they said about working together was right.

Turning back to the wall, he sank down beneath the

ring where his chain was fastened. Elinor followed. She seated herself a short distance away. Neither spoke. Darios curled up on the straw and tried to sleep.

Every now and then, Brak glanced over at Runga. The smith's big dark eyes gleamed in the reflected light from the outer corridor.

Better, perhaps, if he'd killed Runga a while ago, Brak thought. The smith's fascination with Nordica could be a serious threat.

All at once Brak laughed to himself. A threat to what?

For him to believe that they had any real chance at escaping from this dungeon was lunacy. The walls were solid. The chains were stoutly forged.

For a while Brak and Elinor conversed in whispers. He told her a bit more of what he'd learned of Nordica's plans. Elinor in turn narrated the story of how she'd been kidnapped by the red-haired woman's riders. Presently the door-lock rattled.

Two soldiers appeared, one carrying a lantern.

The first soldier prodded Brak's powerful chest with the point of his spear.

"Stand up, yellow-hair. We've instructions to bring you to the lady again."

"I thought we'd settled everything between us."

"That is for Lady Nordica to decide." To his companion, the soldier added, "Unlock the ring from the wall block. To take him we'll have to take the girl too."

At the wall the second guard inserted a large brazen key in an aperture below the fastening ring. Brak frowned.

Why must Elinor accompany him? Surely the soldiers could easily unfasten the wrist cuffs. But he had no time to puzzle over the matter.

The soldiers freed Brak and the girl. He put an arm across Elinor's trembling shoulders as they started out. One guard carried the end of the wall chain, the other the lantern.

Runga glared as Brak left. Again Brak marveled at the smith's blindness. That he should actually desire Nordica was unthinkable.

"Take the tunnel on the left," the guard instructed. "The one leading downward."

"Downward?" Brak said. "I thought we were on the lowest level already."

The guard didn't reply.

Elinor glanced at Brak. She too sensed the strangeness of the situation. As they descended along the sloping floor, tiny red eyes peered at them from dim niches in the tunnel walls. There was a grisly chattering. In one of the niches Brak thought he saw something like a small semi-human face. A statue of some kind? They passed on too quickly for him to be sure.

Why had Nordica summoned them to the very bottom of the castle? Her audience hall was on an upper level. Brak's suspicion mounted with every step.

After seemingly interminable windings, the tunnel straightened out. Here the torch cressets were far apart. The warm air smelled dank. Iridescent bluish mold sprouted in the cracks of the walls. Ahead Brak glimpsed an oblong of light.

A thick oak doorway stood half open. The guards thrust Brak ahead roughly. He stumbled over a length of the chain, spilling into the chamber on all fours. Elinor cried out as the chain pulled sharply on her arm.

Brak raised his head.

The first thing he saw was a gaping black hole in the wall. The hole was tall as a man and twice as wide. From it blew a stench both foul and familiar.

A massive round stone had been rolled away from the opening by means of a log lever and rock fulcrum arrangement. Brak heard the scraping of silken slippers, whipped his head around—

To stare into the dark eyes of Tamar Zed.

The Magian strode forward. "A little stratagem, barbarian. Nordica Fire-Hair is sleeping now. By the time you're gone, she'll be unable to do a thing about it."

Elinor ran to Brak's side, terrified. "The soldiers told you it was Nordica waiting."

"A lie," Brak said. "The Magian is Nordica's lover but his fine lady smiled at me. Even though I'd never touch her, there is such jealousy in him that he has to resort to this kind of trick to get rid of me."

But Brak's jibes only made the dark-bearded Magian smile all the more. Finally Brak spat:

"Very well, Magian. Kill me and have done."

Tamar Zed shook his head. "Not quite yet."

He strolled to the opening in the wall, rapped his knuckles against the round stone.

"In truth, I don't intend to touch you at all. Do you see these two excellent soldiers? A pair of purses has sworn them to silence about the night's work. I'll have them put you into the passage yonder. They'll roll the stone in place. The passage is the same one down which Nordica and I sent old Celsus. Some say it runs to the very bottom of the earth. Down there in the dark, you can commune with the bones of the alchemist until you starve or go mad. A fitting end."

Brak shook his head, amazed. "You'd risk Nordica's wrath to be rid of me?"

"I'd risk things ten times worse to have her to myself."

"Then you're more depraved than I thought," was Brak's sullen reply.

The Magian's cheek flushed with color. "Ignorant clod! What do you know about her power—?"

"I know that for some reason it grips you the way a hawk's claw grips a tiny fledgling. A fledgling can't fight. A man can."

Some awful shadow flickered across the Magian's eyes. "You piece of dung! You have no notion of the holds on a man—"

"Holds strong enough to make a man grovel?" Brak broke in.

"I do what is necessary in her presence—" Tamar blustered.

"Even when that includes crawling in humiliation?"

"There are reasons!" Tamar's tone screamed but the voice was low.

"There is no power in hell or anyplace else strong enough to bind a man's spirit unless he *wills* it bound!"

All at once Tamar Zed's fury seemed to drain away. His mouth contorted in a weak, almost helpless smile. The shadow deepened across his eyes and a ghastly slackness marred his mouth.

86

"You don't know, outlander," he said. "You don't know."

Uneasy silence.

Tamar brushed at his sweat-shining cheek. He blinked several times. He indicated Brak's wrist cuffs, addressing the soldiers:

"Unlock him and put him in the tunnel."

The soldiers glided forward. One pulled a dagger, touched it to Elinor's throat. The warning was clear —should Brak struggle, the knife would slip instantly into her neck.

Aching with fury yet unwilling to risk having the shepherd girl killed, Brak stood like a great stricken beast while the key twisted and the cuff dropped off. From a dark corner of the chamber Tamar Zed returned with something long and glittering resting on his palms. With surprise Brak saw that it was his own broadsword.

"Take this, barbarian," said the Magian, eyes shining. "Take it with you down to wherever that passage leads. Then you can spend the rest of your days proving your bravery by dueling with the darkness."

Tamar spun to the soldiers.

"Throw him in!"

Swiftly the soldiers moved. One still held Elinor's arm. Brak was pushed past the massive stone into the black passage. Tamar flung the broadsword at his feet. Metal rang.

"I'll take the dagger," the Magian said, slipping up behind Elinor.

While he kept guard on her, the two soldiers sprang to the log lever. They leaned their weight on it. With a ponderous creaking and grinding of smaller rocks beneath, the stone began to roll.

Tamar leaned around Elinor from behind. He whispered something to her. The girl turned scarlet.

Laughing, the Magian called for the cuff keys. One of the soldiers threw the ring to him. Tamar caught it deftly, slipped the appropriate key into Elinor's cuff. A moment later her fetters fell away.

Now Brak had the broadsword in his fist. He stood in the dark tunnel watching the edge of the round stone

87

move inexorably across the opening. It was half closed now, the round stone rolled with a grinding that grew steadily louder.

Brak's fingers ached on the sword haft. He longed to plunge back into that chamber, spit the soldiers and the Magian. Yet Tamar's knife trembled close to Elinor's throat. And his sibilant voice reached into the dark:

"—and when the stone is rolled into place, perhaps I can amuse myself with you, girl. Nordica hasn't been kindly to me of late. Nor overly generous. Would you object if I—?"

The rest of the words were muffled as Tamar again bent near Elinor's ear. His free hand slid up her bare arm, then over, for an unwelcome caress.

The monster rock rolled on; the opening was three-quarters closed.

Gasping, Elinor pulled away from the Magian. He laughed, whispered to her again.

With a cry of fright and outrage the shepherd girl pulled away and ran.

Tamar flung up his arm. "Stop her!"

Slow to react, the guards blundered against one another. Tamar shifted the dagger point for throwing, flung the knife hard.

But Elinor was swift. The blade flashed over her head, clanged off the wall just as she plunged through the tunnel opening.

"Roll back the rock!" Tamar cried. "Nordica must have the girl for—"

"Lord, it's too late!" a soldier shouted. "The weight of it pushes it onward."

Elinor stumbled against Brak, clutched him for support. The crack of light between stone and wall narrowed . . . narrowed . . . and vanished.

Tamar's furious yells faded. Brak blinked in the dark. He shook Elinor until her crying subsided.

"Girl, we've got to run wherever this tunnel leads. We must get away before they can move the stone again. At least I have the sword. We're better off faring for ourselves then caught in that box of a room. Do you understand me?"

"Y-yes," she replied.

"Then take my hand. I'll lead the way."

Her fingers were chill and trembling. Carefully he extended his bare foot over the slippery tunnel floor. He took a step. Another.

He moved as rapidly as he could in this fashion, thrusting ahead with the broadsword, testing each new step in case they came to a sudden drop-off.

"The Magian said this tunnel ran down to the earth's core," Elinor breathed.

Brak sniffed the black air. "Or a place far worse."

"What do you mean?"

"Never mind."

They hurried on, Brak balancing carefully between the need for haste and the necessity to avoid any sudden pitfalls. Once, far behind, he thought he heard shouting, oaths, even footfalls, as though the stone had been removed and men were giving chase. He faced about, listening.

Presently the noises died. Evidently Tamar Zed and his bribed helpers had decided against pursuit.

All of a sudden Brak was not so certain that he would not have preferred returning to the room, and fighting.

The warm-blood stench grew more overpowering every second. Brak tapped his way along the passage wall. The floor continued to slope downward through utter darkness.

Then, abruptly, his outstretched sword touched emptiness. His right foot skidded.

"*Back!*"

His cry was lost in the rattle of rocks dislodged into space.

Elinor pulled hard on his arm, spilling them both.

Carefully Brak clambered to hands and knees. He extended his hand.

The tunnel had ended in a narrow ledge along a rock face. They had nearly blundered off into nothingness.

Panting, Brak stood up slowly. "This is where they must have disposed of Celsus the alchemist. Not by murder. By imprisonment. Slow death in a cave leading to nowhere. Or perhaps he fell down to—to—"

Words strangled in his throat. Without quite realizing

it, he had grown aware of a faint light all about them. He raised his head toward its source.

Far above, the dim radiance filtered through what must be a round opening at the surface of the earth. As they huddled on the ledge, Brak closed his hand convulsively over Elinor's. His belly grew cold with fear.

"No wonder Celsus Hyrcanus never came back, girl. The Magian had no idea where the tunnel led. But now I do."

"Brak, listen! Down below. Noises——"

"The rocks I kicked over have wakened it," Brak whispered. The broadsword hung in his hand, seeming as light as some child's toy. "I should have recognized the stench. We're——"

But he could not bring himself to say the words aloud to her. Instead, he peered over the ledge rim.

Below, two great red eyes opened.

Elinor saw them. In a moment she recognized them. She bit her lip and moaned.

The eyes shone, growing larger every instant.

Like a thing out of hell the monster lifted its head on its long, scaly and incredibly supple neck. Huge white jaws lined with spear-like teeth glistened in the dim light from high above.

For an awful moment Brak felt totally helpless. Terror overwhelmed him. He watched, horribly fascinated, afraid, as that ghastly head rose toward them.

Rose higher.

And higher.

And higher——

The Manworm was stirring, to deal with the puny creatures who had disturbed its slumber.

Chapter VII

PRISONERS IN THE PIT

Elinor the shepherd girl had recognized the creature into whose lair the Magian had unwittingly thrust them. Her fingers constricted on the barbarian's thick forearm.

She pressed close against him. Her face was a terror-mask in the weak light drifting down from the opening of the Manworm's cave at the earth's surface, far overhead.

The shepherd girl began to whimper.

"Be silent, girl! Perhaps if we make no outcry, the creature will never see us."

But Elinor had seen far too much herself. Before Brak could prevent her, she screamed.

Her whole body trembled violently. As she lunged against Brak for protection, she kicked several small stones on the ledge. The stones showered off the rim into the chasm.

Too late, Brak clapped his free hand over Elinor's mouth to stifle her shrieks. The girl struggled against the grip of his heavy palm. She twisted, moaned, bit his hand.

Brak's temper blazed up. He shook the girl roughly, his voice low but savage:

"*I say keep silent!* You've already roused the beast with your racket."

Elinor's eyes flew wide open. She understood at last what he was saying. She gave another low moan, nodded weakly. Brak relaxed his grip a little.

Suddenly the walls of the chasm seemed to give off a rumbling sound. The ledge rocked as the Manworm lashed out with its great tail.

The creature's putrefying stink floated everywhere. Elinor's sobbing died. Brak released her, thrust her back against the wall of the narrow ledge.

91

Then he took careful hold of the haft of his broadsword. He leaned forward to peer over the ledge.

The Manworm's head on its long, scaled neck, seemed to be rising like a hideous cloud. The skull of the thing looked to be three times as long as Brak himself was tall. Within the skull oval black-pupilled eyes shone, a deep and luminous scarlet.

The yellow-haired barbarian couldn't be sure what kind of body the Manworm possessed. Most of the creature was hidden by the darkness below. Probably it was long and serpent-like. He glimpsed two supple forepaws, each armored with a dozen claws as big as scythes. The creature used these claws to grasp the chasm wall and lift itself.

The Manworm rose, the scaled head turned and the red eyes searched the gloom.

Now the Manworm's head was almost level with the ledge. The creature let out another of its shattering bellows, so loud Brak's ears ached.

The mammoth tail came lashing up from the darkness. It whipped back and forth in rage, striking the pit walls and sending tremors through the entire cavern. Brak felt the ledge shiver beneath his feet. A narrow fissure perhaps as long as his arm opened in its surface.

The Manworm's head was directly opposite the shelf. Brak pressed back against Elinor, his face turned outward toward the monster. Cold perspiration bathed him as he held the broadsword ready. Like a statue he crouched there, barely breathing.

The Manworm's head darted forward.

Its huge jaws opened to reveal teeth sharp and long as spears. A gust of rotted air clouded out of its mouth, making Brak's belly turn over.

The Manworm dipped its head at the edge of the shelf as though sniffing. Behind Brak, Elinor began to moan again, softly but uncontrollably.

He dared not turn to silence her. The slightest movement might attract the beast's attention.

She moaned louder. Louder still—

The Manworm bellowed again. The red eyes blazed as bright as beacons, so close to Brak and the girl that the barbarian could have extended his right arm and touched

92

the scaly snout with his blade.

Behind the monster's head, its great tail waved in the air. Abruptly the tail struck at the chasm's opposite wall in a whiplash of anger. A crash—and from higher in the cavern more rocks tumbled down. The whole earth seemed to shake.

The dislodged boulders tumbled down on the Manworm's head.

Enraged, the thing reared still higher on its serpentine neck. It bellowed, hitting out with its tail.

The rock-shower diverted the thing long enough for Brak to whirl and clap his hand across Elinor's mouth again. Wrenched into this awkward position and breathing between clenched teeth, he heard the rocks clatter to the bottom of the pit.

A moment later, the Manworm's head began to sink down. The head dropped below the ledge.

For long, agonized moments Brak kept his hand pressed tight against the girl's lips. He prayed that the falling rocks had caused the Manworm to miss seeing its prey. A weird, echoing bellow from some distance below soon told Brak that this was the case.

He released Elinor. "No sound yet! Else it'll rear up again. If it doesn't we may be safe a while."

Bracing his palms against the ledge, he leaned forward to look over.

The ground-level opening at the roof of the pit was so far away that the light here was weak, deceptive. Yet Brak thought he could make out great glistening coils folding and re-folding upon themselves. The two red eyes floated like bloody lanterns below.

Presently the eyes narrowed, as though lid-membranes were sliding shut. In a moment the eyes went black altogether.

Breath whistled out through the big barbarian's lips. He was bathed in chilly sweat. He managed a smile he did not feel.

"Girl? You can sit up now. The hell-thing's gone back to sleep."

Elinor sat up. Her trembling stopped. But her cheeks still were white.

"How long will it sleep?" she whispered.

93

"I can't say. Perhaps long enough for us to try to get out of this hole. Now if we—what's wrong?"

Elinor was shaking her head. "I can't. I have no strength left."

Angrily he seized her shoulder. "Would you rather wait here till it comes for us?"

"No, Brak. But the way is closed. Tamar Zed's men rolled the great stone into place." She indicated the blackness further back along the ledge, the ending of the tunnel down which the Magian had thrust them.

Brak used his broadsword to point overhead. "That way is open."

"How can we reach it?"

"Climb," he replied grimly. "Up the wall of the pit and out."

The thought of such an effort started Elinor crying again. Rubbed raw by the terror of the last few moments, Brak shoved her back against the ledge wall.

"Mewling and moaning won't do any good, girl! Either we try to flee while the thing sleeps or we remain and let it devour us. Or, if it never finds us, we starve. Which prospect appeals to you most? I say we should take the chance. Try to climb."

Controlling herself with effort, Elinor nodded. "All —all right, I'll try."

"Rest a moment or two. Then we'll start." Brak stood up, leaned his broadsword against the ledge wall. "In a crevice back there I saw growing things. Wait."

Testing the fissured surface with every step, the barbarian moved warily down the ledge until he reached the cleft in the wall. Damp, green plants with fluffy stalks grew there.

Brak tore out several of the stalks. He sniffed them. He crushed a bit of one in his palm. He munched on it. The fiber was sweet, relatively tender. After a moment he ate a bit more.

Satisfied, he gathered all he could find and carried the plants back to Elinor.

"Fit to be eaten, I think. Take some. It may give you a little strength."

Seeming to welcome some commonplace, physical act like eating, the shepherd girl crushed several stalks the way he showed her, and ate. Brak's belly no longer rumbled quite so emptily either. A measure of calm returned to both of them.

Finally Elinor brushed at a lock of the long brown hair that had fallen across her cheek.

"How far is it to the top, Brak?"

"We mustn't think that way, girl. Else we'll never get out. Just tell yourself it's not so far, and a strong man and a strong woman can make it. Tear off a strip of the hem of your gown. I want to tie up a sling for the sword."

The girl turned her back. Her modesty brought a faint smile to the lips of the brawny man. That Elinor would fall back into a habit of feminine shyness at such a moment was a hopeful sign.

He glanced down into the pit again. Total darkness. Only the powerful decayed smell served as a reminder that the Manworm slept in the blackness. No doubt the slightest sound would rouse it again. And climbing up would be noisy.

Still, they couldn't afford to remain on the ledge, starving or going out of their minds or both. That was precisely what Tamar Zed wanted. Brak had scores to settle with the Magian now, as well as with Nordica Fire-Hair.

Elinor handed Brak the strip of cloth. He tied it to the broadsword hilt, then also around his left shoulder.

"Ready," he said.

"Where do we begin?"

"Yonder, on the left. See that outcrop? The cavern wall looks rough from that point upward. Let me go first." He gripped Elinor's hand briefly, trying to give her reassurance he himself did not feel. "Hold to the lion-hide around my middle. I'll support us both as we climb."

She tried to smile. She couldn't.

Straining outward with his left arm, Brak reached for the outcrop. He stepped across the short gap between the ledge and the boss-like thrust of stone on which he found a foothold.

Seizing the rock wall with his left hand, he extended his right hand back to Elinor.

She grasped his wrist, jumped across. Landing, she stumbled against him. For a moment both the girl and the barbarian were in danger of teetering into space.

95

But Brak held fast to the wall, muscles twisting and bunching in his mighty shoulders. Elinor gripped the lion-hide tied tightly around his belly. When they had both regained balance, she drew back.

Elinor forced a smile. This time, though, her eyes shone with a little courage, a little hope. The first small step to the outcrop had demonstrated that they did have a chance to survive.

Brak smiled in return. It was hollow optimism, though. The cavern wall stretched far, far upward. The dim opening at ground level was a mere blur of grayish radiance. With a growl Brak grasped the stones over his head and pulled himself upward.

A moment later he drew Elinor up behind him. He climbed again.

How much time passed in that frightful ascent, Brak was unable to say. They moved cautiously. He tested each handhold and foothold. Their line of climb was not direct. Many times they were forced to move left or right around the tunnel wall to find the next secure step.

After a bit Brak's huge arms began to ache. He said nothing. The dim light far above began to seem unreachable.

Resting on another narrow ledge, Brak panted, "How are you faring, girl?"

"I hurt. Every part of me hurts."

"Can you keep going?"

"We've come this far. We can go the rest."

"Good," was all he answered.

Lost in the alien cave where the Manworm slept, abandoned by their enemies and facing obstacles to which many a saner man would have surrendered without a struggle, Brak suddenly felt a burst of affection for the slim, shy girl. He reached out clumsily. On the high steppes, where he had been born, fine manners were unknown. He laid his palm against her cheek.

Elinor's flesh felt warm. She closed her hand over his fingers. Then, embarrassed, she let go.

Brak laughed low. The new feeling of comradeship with the girl lent him added strength.

"We're nearly halfway up," he said. "Just there—see where that black shadow juts? I think it's another ledge. It

96

looks big. We'll go that far, then rest."

Elinor nodded. Brak stood, lifted his right leg to climb to the next little thrust of rock.

The large shelf was not more than twice his own height above them. It seemed a simple matter to reach it now. When they did, the perilous climb would be half-finished.

Brak brought Elinor up beside him. He strained high again, touched the lip of the ledge which extended some distance out into space over his head.

"Difficult," he grumbled. "I'll have to lean backward, then jump and catch it. After I do, you seize hold of my legs. I'll pull us up."

Elinor's intake of breath said that she knew the danger of the maneuver. Brak adjusted the cloth sling holding his broadsword. He swiped his forearm across his mouth. He pushed his yellow hair back from his forehead.

He gathered his legs under him and leaped high.

For one mad instant he had the sensation of sailing helplessly in space high above the sleeping Manworm. Then, with an involuntary yell, he flung his hands out and caught the ledge.

His left hand slipped.

He held on with his right. His muscles wrenched and writhed. He dangled in space, supported only by five fingers.

Gradually, with great exertion, he brought his left hand back up. He clung to the ledge and called:

"Now, girl. Jump and catch my legs."

As he called it he tensed, waiting for the added weight. It struck him suddenly, a dragging weight that threatened to pull him into the void.

"Brak? Brak, I can't hold on—*I'm slipping down*—"

He felt it. Her arms, wrapped around his mighty legs, were sliding.

He dug his upper teeth into his lip. Slowly, slowly, with inhuman effort, he began to draw himself upward.

His forehead cleared the rim of the ledge.

Then his chin.

But Elinor's weight was pulling on him. His strength was failing. She was slipping faster.

Higher Brak pulled himself—

Higher—

Now his neck cleared the rim.

His chest.

His belly.

Elinor screamed softly, slipped again.

Brak slammed his head and chest forward, striking hard against the surface of the ledge. Doubled over, he lay that way only an instant. He began to hitch his body forward.

"Get one hand on the edge," he croaked. "Then I can drag you up."

Elinor let out a low sob. Brak felt her weight shift. He wrenched his head around, saw white fingers straining for purchase on the ledge.

The moment she caught hold of it, he flung his legs up and over so that his whole body was on the shelf. At the same time he grabbed frantically at Elinor's arm, just as her right hand slipped and she started to drop.

But he had her.

First by one arm.

Then by both.

A moment later, weak with exertion, he lifted the shepherd girl to safety on the wide ledge. Panting and shuddering uncontrollably, they lay side by side a long time.

* * *

At last Brak rose to survey the shelf.

It was roughly triangular. Its two upper sides converged into a patch of darkness at the rear. The black was even more stygian than the rest of the pit.

Brak wondered whether the intense dark might be the mouth of a cave. About to take a step in that direction to find out, he went rigid.

"*Elinor?*" He whispered it without turning. "Lie very still. Something is breathing back there."

There was no mistake. He heard the sibilance clearly.

Carefully Brak unslung the broadsword, braced his legs wide. Their noise climbing up must have roused whatever thing dwelled in the shelf cave.

In addition to a rush of breath, there was an abrupt shuffling, a slithering, as of someone or something crawling out of its den.

Brak took a step forward, dropped into a crouch—

With a flapping, a screeching, a rush of moldy air, the apparition hurled out of the cave.

Claws raked Brak's cheek. Musty cloth whipped around him.

Blinded by the flapping cloths, Brak fastened both hands on the sword haft. He swung the blade back over his head for a downstroke that would cleave the thing in half.

"Don't!" Elinor screamed. *"It's only an old man!"*

Savagely the barbarian wrenched the sword aside, leaped back. His spine scraped the ledge wall. The thing that had come stumbling from the cave was outlined against the dim radiance filtering from overhead. Brak goggled.

The tottering human skeleton was incredibly filthy. His eyebrows and beard were white, tangly forests. His flapping robes were no more than long tatters of cloth. On one of the tatters Brak glimpsed a faded crescent moon sewn with tarnished gilt thread.

Tiny eyes all but buried in wrinkled, filthy-yellow skin darted back and forth from Brak's broadsword to his face. The apparition was apparently terrified for its life. It made a moaning sound, *"Uhhh, uhhh, uhhh."*

The barbarian's spine crawled. He thought he knew the human horror's name.

"Alchemist?" he whispered.

"Uhhh."

"Celsus Hyrcanus?"

The old man waved his arms as if to ward off blows. *"Uhhh! Uhhh!"*

"Alchemist, listen! This girl and I won't harm you."

The trembling figure spoke words that sounded like, "Begone! Begone, I know you not."

"We were cast down here by the same enemies who betrayed you. The Magian—"

Spittle bubbled to the cracked lips. He waved his arms about once more. "Tamar's his name. Evil, evil—like you."

"Yes, Tamar. He put us here. He's in league with your daughter."

"Not mine!" the old man screeched with piercing

clarity. "Not mine now! She became possessed. Evil took her—evil made my daughter into—*uhhh, uhhhh!*"

The old man covered his hairy face with his hands, as though memory of Nordica Fire-Hair was too awful.

Brak swiped at his mouth. He gnawed his underlip and thought about the words the old man had wheezed out a moment before.

Nordica became possessed.

Possessed by what—or whom?

Once more the premonition of immense evil engulfed him. He thought of the face of Ariane.

Impossible! She was dead.

But hadn't the Nestorians told him that the evil of Yob-Haggoth and his minions could only slumber, never die? The mysterious rockslide—the curious mockery in the eyes of Nordica Fire-Hair—the consuming certainty that he'd seen her somewhere before—and now this ruined horror of a man saying that his daughter had been taken over by some outside power. It all formed a sinister pattern.

The skeleton-figure was crooning at him again. "You are—*uhhh*—enemies too—*begone!*"

"We're not enemies," Brak insisted.

The apparition howled and waggled its arms. "*Uhhh! Uhhh!*"

Brak tried one last time. He extended his hand slowly.

The old man scrabbled back against the wall, drooling and mewing. His eyes were tiny wet highlights in the shadow that surrounded him.

From behind the big barbarian, Elinor breathed:

"Is it really the alchemist?"

"Look at the sun- and moon-signs stitched on his robe."

"Then he's alive, Brak!"

"Evidently neither the witch-woman nor the Magian understood clearly that the tunnel led into this pit. That's one explanation. Or they did know and it suited them to thrust the old man down here to die of abandonment and starvation. In any event he survived long enough to reach this ledge. Doubtless those plants we gnawed on, or similar ones, have sustained him. Sustained his body, I mean. The rest of him—his mind—"

Brak's face wrenched as he turned to indicate Celsus Hyrcanus. The movement frightened the man.

"*Uhhh, uhhh, uhhh!*"

Voice rising into a shriek, the apparition stepped away from the wall. The old man jiggled his arms franticallly. For a moment his face was more fully illuminated. With horror Brak saw that the few patches of skin not concealed by the beard were covered with unwholesome grayish-green sores.

Out of the old man's face the tiny eyes gleamed with the terror of one whose mindless domain has been invaded. Moment by moment his moans grew louder.

"We won't harm you, old one," Brak began again. "If you'd only listen to me—"

The man paid no attention. He stumbled forward:

"*Begone, begone!*"

"Celsus Hyrcanus!" Brak roared. "We're your friends. We'll take you out of here!"

"No use," Elinor exclaimed. "There's nothing left in his skull but terrors."

Finally Brak saw it was true. The pitiful creature shambled ahead step by infantile step. His long-grown fingernails raked the air with slashing strokes. He kept repeating that dreadful senseless cry. The only real instinct still stirring in his mind must be the dim one that prodded him to protect his fouled nesting-place on the ledge.

Abruptly the barbarian realized how loudly Celsus Hyrcanus was yelling. His insides knotted up.

Far below, there was a rumbling. An abortive bellow.

No time to scruple now. Brak raced forward, locked his elbow around the alchemist's scrawny neck.

"Be silent!" Brak cried, wrestling the man toward the cave.

The alchemist was surprisingly strong. In his slashing hands and kicking legs he had the power of the demented. The blows angered Brak:

"Be silent, I said! You'll rouse the beast sleeping down there and we'll all be—"

The shelf shook. A sound of thunderous lashing rose from the dark.

Celsus seemed to stiffen in Brak's grasp, as if he too understood the nature of the sound.

Drool glistened on the old man's lips. He repeated one word.

"Manworm."

Bellow followed bellow. Brak thrust the alchemist away, cursed in despair. Elinor ran back from the lip of the ledge. Brak's sword-arm felt heavy, tired.

Celsus lurched back into his cave. But his cries persisted. They rang from the shelf walls until the bellows of the Manworm drowned them out.

Brak took up a position at the shelf edge. To Elinor he said:

"Get behind me. Stay hidden."

The red eyes in the great head were rising swiftly out of the dark now. The tail lashed furiously at the pit walls.

This time there was no avoiding the battle.

Chapter VIII

SWORD AND DEMON

Not a few strange, awesome sights in unfamiliar lands had startled and amazed Brak in his journey to Khurdisan in the south. But all these past experiences were forgotten in the moment when he stood on the ledge watching the Manworm rise from the darkness.

The stench gusting from the creature's open jaws was the smell of earth itself, but earth decayed through endless centuries. The smell was overpowering, sickening.

Indeed, compared with the huge beast from the pit, Brak seemed a puny figure despite his big size. He stood with powerful legs wide apart, head slightly lowered, eyes glaring warily down at the clawed serpent-thing.

Then, as though he'd taken a cooling draught of wine, he lifted his chin. And laughed, low and harshly.

He hitched up the garment of lion's hide about his hips, chuckled again. True, he was afraid. But he realized that he'd probably lost his life anyway the moment Tamar Zed decided to cast him into the tunnel. Therefore, with life worthless, he needn't let the fear of losing it hamper him when the Manworm attacked.

Behind him, Elinor clung to the shelf wall. The mad moanings of old Celsus issued from the cave into which the alchemist had fled. The Manworm was nearly up to Brak's level—

The huge serpent-thing could not immediately locate its prey. The scaled tail flicked back and forth, back and forth. That tail was so long and strong that each flick against the sides of the cavern dislodged great chunks of slate, sent them thundering down into the depths.

As its great red eyes came up level with the shelf, the Manworm bellowed. From the open jaws and between the fangs that were as long as a man is tall, a wet-dripping tongue uncoiled, triple-forked at the end.

The tongue shot out between the jaws as if hoping to snatch some morsel from the air. Brak hauled his broadsword back over his shoulder. Hot excitement churned inside him. The triple fork was questing blindly. The beast still didn't know that Brak was on the shelf, quite close.

The tongue reached nearer.

Nearer.

In the heartbeats before the Manworm would finish its bellow and the fully extended tongue would start to draw back, Brak cut downward with his blade.

He put all the power of his great arm behind the blow.

The Manworm sensed the stirring in the air as the blade flashed. Its eyes grew a deeper scarlet in an instant. Its long, tubular neck twisted. The head swung around, instinctively jerking back from the sudden agony of naked metal hacking into its tongue-flesh.

Brak's blade sliced deep. The cutting edge bit the suety surface of the tongue forks. Two of the three forks dropped off. From their roots blackish ichor, putrescent, sprayed over Brak.

The Manworm saw him then. Saw and knew that Brak

104

was the tiny thing which caused him so much pain.

Back against the cavern's opposite wall the Manworm reared, bellowing, *bellowing*—

The roar was so thunderous, Brak felt as though a spike had pierced his brain. The droplets of ichor on his flesh stung, burned. He leaped back from the edge as the Manworm struck the far cavern wall, then shot its head forward on the long neck.

More ichor showered over him, hellishly painful. The stuff still fountained from the hacked tongue. The Manworm lashed its tail side to side in steady rhythm, an indication of its mounting rage. The roar in the cavern was continuous.

Retreating, Brak watched the tongue shoot forth again. It twitched across onto the shelf, like an exploring hand. He raised his sword for another blow, yelled in alarm as his foot skidded in a pool of the monster's black life-fluid.

Somewhere in the dark Elinor saw Brak go down. She screamed.

The Manworm's tongue slid across Brak's belly. It slipped down over his ribs and twitched beneath him. It coiled and coiled, winding around his middle like a great rope. Clouds of foul air from the beast's gullet washed over him.

Chopping futilely with the sword, Brak was picked up by that huge enwrapping tongue and lifted across the edge of the shelf.

He was carried through the air toward the Manworm's jaws. Rows of fangs seemed to rush toward him. The tongue threatened to crush the life from him. In another instant, he would either be broken in half or sucked down inside those gigantic jaws, which were already beginning to close.

Brak was over the pit now, burning from head to foot with the ichor that leaked from the severed forks. Closer the jaws loomed. *Closer*—

Brak twisted. His upper body ached with unbearable agony. But he managed to clamp both hands on the broadsword and hold it high. He aimed the point at a pinkish-white ridge of cartilage just above the sockets of the Manworm's great upper fangs. His life was done if

that ridge was as bony-hard as it looked in the failing light—

Brak braced his body for the contact of the sword point against the cartilage. Just as the tongue dragged him between those white, dripping fangs, the broadsword struck and dug in.

The tongue constricted, tightening around his belly. Wildly he kicked. His naked soles slipped on the rough, damp surface of two of the huge lower fangs.

Exerting every ounce of strength, feeling his eyes begin to burn and his temples ache as though the blood would burst out through their bony walls, Brak stiffened his entire body. Legs jammed against two of the beast's lower teeth and broadsword above his head, point buried into the yielding cartilage, he became a grisly human wedge holding the Manworm's jaws apart.

Only this backbreaking stance prevented him from being drawn down into the beast's mouth. How long he could stay thus braced was another matter.

The Manworm felt the resistance. The muscles in its tongue began to constrict again.

Brak's belly felt crushed, pulped, awash with hurt. His right foot slipped off the fang against which he braced. Desperately he shifted the foot back, hunting for something to push against.

Instead of exerting a steady pressure, the Manworm began to jerk its tongue rhythmicallly. Each jerk tightened the hellish coils around the barbarian's midsection. He shouted aloud in agony.

He could stay in his present position just a moment more. Any longer and his spine would snap.

He resisted the tremendous pressure of the next rhythmic constriction around his middle. Then, as the tongue relaxed briefly, Brak jerked the broadsword out of the jaw cartilage. He slashed it downward into the central stalk of the tongue itself.

The Manworm reared again. Brak was nearly blinded by the reddish light spilling from the beast's eyes. But he knew he'd scored a wound on the tongue-stalk. Once more his legs were awash with stinging ichor.

The coiled pressure around his middle relaxed still further. Hacking and gouging with the broadsword, Brak pushed himself upward through the coils. His hips came free. Then his entire lower body. The tongue was beginning to droop.

Brak leaped high. He caught the beast's snout, a horny protrusion big as a small burial hill. He went scrambling up the spine that ran along the middle of the snout.

Again the Manworm wrenched its head. Brak was hurled against a plate-like place directly between the scarlet eyes. The scales of the hide were large enough to give him a handhold, though. He clung to one of them while the Manworm hurled itself from side to side in torment.

The great head dipped, swayed, bucked. To either side the huge scarlet eyes burned, reddish ovals twice Brak's height. Like a tenacious insect he held on to the scales between those eyes while the Manworm tried to shake off the irritant it knew was crouching on the crest of its snout.

Almost mad with the delirium of the struggle, Brak breathed in wild gulps. His body ached in a hundred places. Yet he couldn't flag now, and he wouldn't. A berserker's rage filled him, and he became a beast with only one aim, that of the Manworm—to kill its enemy.

The Manworm's convulsions dislodged more large stones. They sailed down into the pit with mighty crashes. The entire cavern was trembling. The light had grown dimmer. Suddenly Brak saw a chance for victory.

If he could slide over to one of the great eyes and ram his broadsword into the socket, he might strike the brain.

The black ichor covering his body reflected the baleful scarlet glare of those eyes. Carefully Brak fastened his left hand on one of the scales. He moved a step closer to the right eye.

Although the Manworm's hide was tough, it seemed to have its own bizarre sensitivity. Brak's moving foot somehow told the creature where its quarry was. Out of the pit rose one of the monster's forepaws.

The other paw had fastened around the edge of the shelf where Brak had begun his battle. The paw traveling through the air twisted inward. Brak slammed himself back against the scaly wall between the Manworm's eyes as twelve scythe-like claws closed slowly, reaching to pluck him from his hiding place.

The claws formed a white circle of sharp points, raked suddenly down the Manworm's snout. The claw-tips gouged the armored hide but missed Brak.

Again the Manworm tore at its own snout. It struck blindly, hoping to snare the thing it felt but could not see. One of the claws grazed Brak's right thigh, opening a long gash.

A third time the claws raked down. They missed Brak by the barest margin. Brak realized that the longer he waited, crushed back against the scales, the smaller became his chances of living to deliver a mortal blow.

The Manworm drew its paw away in preparation for another strike. Its bellowing deepened amid the thunder of tumbling rocks. Before the paw came slashing in again, Brak leaped at the right eye.

His toe caught in a joint between scales. He pitched forward. The claw descended—

Like a projectile from a siege machine, one of the falling boulders struck the monster's paw. The Manworm screamed. The claws opened, clamped shut frantically on empty air. The rock, which the beast had mistaken for Brak himself, went tumbling on down into the dark.

Spared a moment longer, Brak used the opportunity to brace his legs beneath him. He sprang forward with his right arm thrust out. The broadsword shimmered like fire, reflecting red light from the great eye—

The point struck hard scales.

Brak wrenched to the side, driving in with all his might. Suddenly the sword-tip scraped across one more scale and slid into the soft joining at the edge of the socket.

With a maddened scream of triumph Brak grasped the haft with both hands and rammed deep. He pushed the weapon in up to its hilt, twisting at the same time.

The right eye, so ruby-bright a moment ago, began to flow beneath the surface of its membrane with a black cloudiness. The killing stroke drove the Manworm into a violent upward convulsion.

Higher shot the Manworm's head, up through the cavern. The beast arched in ultimate pain. Brak grappled to hang onto the scale between the eyes. The other, left eye was also darkening.

At the height of its arc the Manworm let out a bellow louder than any that had preceded it. The cavern seemed to crumble on all sides.

Beneath Brak's feet the snout scales were awash with ichor that flowed out around the hilt of his sword. Brak slipped, tumbled as the Manworm plunged downward again, trying by its convulsions to free itself of the iron spike imbedded through its eye into its brain.

Down it fell, down. Brak was hurled into space, no hand- or footholds left, only the spinning dark.

He had won, yet he was finished. The Manworm had flung him off. He would die somewhere in the bowels of the pit, crushed beneath the stinking carcass that was collapsing, falling like a juggernaut.

Suddenly Brak's legs struck something firm but slime-covered. He threw his arms out wildly, closed them around it. He was whipped from side to side. His head jerked until he thought his neck would break.

Through his pain and confusion he understood that he'd caught hold of the Manworm's tail. But the tail, like the creature, was dying in a demented frenzy. Brak was carried toward the side of the cavern by the lashing tail. In an instant more, he would be pulped—

The moment before the tail struck the rock wall, Brak let go.

The force of the tail's swing threw him wide. He slammed against rock with brutal force. By sheer instinct alone he fought for a grip as his legs dropped from beneath him.

With a violent motion he dragged his knees up onto the knoblike protrusion of rock onto which he'd fallen. He thrust his fingers into a tiny crevice, wedged them there despite the pain.

He closed his eyes and hung on.

Jagged boulders still plummeted through the darkness. But the Manworm had fallen far down into the pit now. Its dying red eyes were mere dull spots of radiance without definition. Its bellow sounded feeble.

Presently there was a last crash, a last scaly scrape of the tail against rock far below. The rocks ceased to fall.

110

The grinding roar echoed away to silence. The red lights dimmed and went out.

Cheek against the cold stone, fingers jammed into the crevice, Brak closed his eyes. He let the hot, salt-rich tears of exhaustion and triumph wash down his cheeks.

* * *

When he regained his control, he managed to pull his fingers from the crevice. Driving out all thought of the pain in his body, he began to climb in the general direction of the shelf where he had left Elinor.

He felt terribly alone and helpless in the near-dark. His broadsword was gone. Perhaps he had been mortally hurt. He seemed unable to see clearly whereas, before, the light from the high opening had enabled him to perceive details of the cavern with fair clarity. He climbed mostly by feel and instinct, calling up into the black:

"Elinor?"

Silence. He called her name a second time.

When he had nearly abandoned hope of hearing her voice, thinking perhaps that old Celsus Hyrcanus in his madness had killed her, she replied.

"Brak?"

Quick new strength surged through him. He climbed faster. "Keep shouting, girl. Loudly as you can, so I know where you are."

Somewhere overhead, he heard the shepherd girl's exclamation of surprise and joy.

As he ordered, Elinor cried his name over and over into the chasm. He used the last remaining bits of his strength to make his way up to her.

Suddenly the rock wall flared above him. Elinor's voice sounded very close.

He pulled himself up, flung a leg over. Gasping, he crawled onto the shelf. He stunk of the Manworm's ichor and his own blood and sweat.

The girl shrank from him.

"The thing—perished," he whispered through blood-ied lips. "Now we can—find our way out—out of—"

His skull was full of tiny dancing lights. Waves of pain cascaded over him. A dark gulf widened in his mind,

111

sucked his whole being into it and he rolled over on his great back, unconscious.

When he woke, the big barbarian was conscious of a faint chittering noise. Conscious too of a different feel to his flesh.

With a groan he turned onto his side. He shook his head to clear it. Haggard, pale, Elinor knelt beside him. With her help Brak sat up.

The effort cost him a severe pain or two. Otherwise, all his bones seemed to be in their proper places. He localized the source of the chittering—the cave.

"Is that the alchemist hiding back there in his warren?" he wanted to know.

"Aye, Brak. I called to him for help several times. He wouldn't answer."

"How long have I slept?"

"Many hours, I think. I don't know exactly. I dozed myself, sitting here keeping watch."

She indicated a litter of crumpled moss-like plants near-by, continued:

"I used those to scrub away as much of the black filth as I could. What was the hideous stuff? It was all over you."

"The blood of the Manworm. It flows no more."

He stood up, grasped her hand. He pulled her close to his side and stared up at the dim roof of the cavern. He said nothing about the dimmer light in the pit; it was now hardly light at all. Instead he told her:

"We must try to get out. I'll climb up alone to scout the way. Stay here until I come back."

"No," she said instantly. "Not here, not with that old man hiding."

The mewings and chittering issuing from the cave were a meaningless mockery of human speech. Brak studied Elinor's face as best he could. Her eyes had a faint glassy shine, as though their experiences had been almost more than her mind could bear. Best not to push her.

"Very well," he said tiredly. "We'll both climb up to the next resting place. I'll leave you there and go on alone."

To this Elinor agreed. Brak took her hand, led her over

112

to the shelf's edge. Once more, with the big barbarian leading the way and the girl clinging to his lion-hide garment, they began to make their way upward.

A short distance above the large shelf they found another, narrower one. Here Brak left the girl huddled, setting out to go the rest of the way to the top. His body still ached from the ferocious death-battle with the Manworm. But he dulled the hurt by forcing himself to think of escape, of his own red thirst for revenge against Nordica Fire-Hair and Tamar Zed.

Long before he reached the pit's upper opening, he saw the reason for the dimness of the light.

Heartsick, he climbed the rest of the way. He expended a long time, and many curses, struggling to move a large boulder. It was one of dozens which had tumbled in upon the entrance tunnel. He got nowhere.

He struck his fist against the boulder, damning all the dark gods of the earth. Then, laboriously, he began the downward climb.

When he rejoined Elinor he told her:

"The Manworm's thrashings dislodged much rock. At the top there is only a tiny opening. It's scarcely big enough to poke a hand through. Beyond, in the tunnel leading outside, even more rock has fallen. As nearly as I could tell, the tunnel is blocked for almost its entire length. That is why the light is so feeble now."

Seeing the bleakness of his face, Elinor said, "Then we're imprisoned here after all?"

"Not necessarily. We—"

"Yes we are! Prisoned here till we die!"

"Don't screech at me, girl!"

"I'm afraid, Brak."

"Of what?" he snarled. "The Manworm is dead."

"Of—" A strange, involuntary shudder seemed to wrench her whole body. "—Everything. That mad old man in the cave. The witch-woman. The Magian. It's almost as if evil gods had cursed both of us."

"Nonsense," was Brak's hoarse retort. But he averted his eyes.

In his mind he saw a squatting semi-human figure with brutal stone fists resting upon crossed stone legs and a

113

stone mouth downcurving in malevolence. Great carved stone eyes looked out and saw the evil of their predicament and thought it good—

Why was he tormenting himself with phantoms? Why was he thinking of Yob-Haggoth's idol at a time like this?

There was no sensible reason, none whatever. Yet something disturbed him. Something he had seen or heard in Nordica's keep.

What was it?

His exhausted mind refused to answer. He shook off the puzzle as best he could, because Elinor was plucking at his arm. Tears ran like silver threads down her grimy face:

"I—I've prayed to my gods, Brak. It's done no good."

"Perhaps it helped with the Manworm," he replied cynically.

"We're just as badly off as we were before he attacked."

"At least we're alive. We've come through the worst."

But he was lying, of course. There were huge, sinister forces working, not merely in the cavern, but within the very tissue and texture of Nordica's plottings. Riddles remained to be answereed. Masks remained to be ripped away. He was not certain he wanted it to happen. He lied to Elinor to protect her already battered sensibilities as best he could.

His effort was not a great success. Her hand dug deeper into his thick arm:

"Try praying with me that we'll meet no more perils, Brak."

"But we will, girl. Besides, what good will it do to pray to your puny local deities?"

"Then pray to the greater gods! To any god you care about."

The cruciform of the Nestorians drifted wraithlike across the screen of his mind. In a raw voice he said:

"There are none."

But he almost wished there were.

"What can we do, then, Brak? What can we possibly—?"

His slashing gesture alarmed and silenced her. "If you'd stop that clacking, I might be able to think about that."

114

Elinor sniffled. He muttered an awkward apology.

Mercifully, she did keep silent, and the sense of pervading evil weakened a little under the onslaught of more practical considerations. At length he said:

"There is one thing we might try, though it's a slim hope. And it depends upon how much strength you have left."

"What is it?"

"We could go back through the tunnel into which Tamar Zed put us. We might be able to rouse someone in the castle. Once back with Nordica, our chances for life would be poor. But here, they barely exist at all."

Swiftly Elinor rose. Perhaps extreme terror forced courage upon her, forced her to compose herself and reach a decision:

"Then let's try."

"Not afraid any more?"

"Of—of course I am. But even the castle is better than this ghastly dark."

They climbed down to the large shelf. Brak called into the cave:

"Celsus? Celsus Hyrcanus? We're your friends. We're going to try to return to the house of your daughter Nordica, and deal with her as she deserves. Let us take you along."

The chittering stopped. Then:

"*Uhhh, uhhh!* Begone!"

The chittering resumed.

Elinor and Brak exchanged forlorn looks.

They left the demented old man where he clearly wished to remain, lost in the dark of the pit and the deeper dark of his own tangled brain.

Slowly, painfully, with many rests, the pair scrambled down the rock wall. At last they came to the shelf which led into the tunnel.

The shelf was sheared half away. Probably the result of the Manworm's furious convulsions. The tunnel mouth was partially blocked with rubble, but this they entered without difficulty.

All along the dark passage, stones had fallen and fissures had opened in the walls. After a seemingly in-

115

terminable time, Brak let out a low growl.

Ahead, beyond another pile of fallen rock, yellow light gleamed.

The round stone blocking the entrance to the subterranean room displayed a ragged V-shaped cleft. The Manworm's fury had reached this far, to crack the stone in half.

Turning, Brak looked down at the trembling shepherd girl. The way was open into Nordica's castle.

But now Brak himself hesitated. He was weary. He had no sword. He wasn't sure whether the cracked stone was a blessing or a curse. Beyond it, he might find riddle-answers he did not want to learn, lift masks he did not want to see behind. The effluvium of monstrous and impending evil swirled around him anew—

Then he looked at Elinor's face. He knew his choice.

Life remained. They had to go on.

Grasping the girl's hand, Brak led her forward in silence, through the cracked stone and into the house of their enemies.

Chapter IX

IN THE CATACOMBS OF YOB-HAGGOTH

Brak's eyes swept the corners of the underground room. It was empty.

The lamp had nearly burned out. The wick floated in a tiny pool of oil. Occasionally the flame petered out, only to puff alight again and throw the massive shadow of Brak's shoulders on the damp wall.

The grim lines around the barbarian's mouth relaxed a little.

"The jackals did their work and ran back aboveground to bark about their victory." He pointed to the second of two openings to black, musty-smelling passages. "That must be the way up to the castle. The other one is the entrance through which they brought us here."

"I was too frightened to remember .anything," Elinor admitted.

"We must try to reach the two prisoners still in the dungeon. That one-legged sailor and the other one, Runga the smith—the one I liked very little—have strong fighting arms. Three men together will have a better chance to break out of these walls than one alone."

So saying, Brak started for the left-hand entrance. Elinor followed. Her eyes were uncertain, fearful again.

Due to the slope of the rock floor, their descent to the underground room had been easy. Going upward was more difficult. Brak had only instinct to guide him, his hunter's sense. That sense had often put food in his belly in places where it seemed no animal life could possibly exist.

The path upward was dark and hard. At each junction of stygian stone-walled passages, Brak paused. He breathed sibilantly a moment, sniffed the air. Then he grunted:

"This way."

The duel with the Manworm had taken its toll, however. The more they climbed, the more his mighty legs ached. Elinor fell several times.

Abruptly yellowness shone ahead. Brak pushed Elinor behind him, crept forward. The wall on his left came to an end.

Peering, the barbarian saw a short cross-passage which ended in a stone arch. Beyond the arch, several dim lamps in niches illuminated what appeared to be a large room with walls of stone. His skin crawled inexplicably.

"Some sort of room yonder," he whispered. "Let me look into it."

"I'll go with y—"

"No!"

He was startled at the curtness of his own voice. The sense of evil increased by the moment. His entire body broke out in a chill sweat. He thrust Elinor against the wall at the passage corner and slipped down toward the arch.

His shadow twisted along the rock beside him,

elongated, deformed. His muscles seemed to demand that he drop into a stalking crouch. The yellow braid and lion tail bobbed behind him as he crept along, nostrils enlarged, lips skinned back, eyes blank and murderous. With a sure instinct, he smelled hell-horror just past that arch.

He heard nothing from inside the chamber. In the preternatural stillness, little wisps of smoke from the lamps floated in the air like transparent serpents. Then Brak's nose picked out a strange yet familiar smell.

Carefully he curled his fingers around the edge of the arch. His insides churned because all at once he knew the smell.

People had died in that lamplit chamber. The smell was the reek of old blood.

Quickly he moved forward, crouched to meet an adversary.

The blow was mental rather than physical. His eyes and brain took in the scene in but a heartbeat's time. The walls were old and time-stained, hewn out eons ago, perhaps. By contrast, the square stone altar in the room's center was new.

The altar was pale gray stone shading to white. Dark stains shimmered in the glow of a dozen lamps ranged in the niches. Something that had spilled on the altar's top had leaked over the edges and down the sides in a time not long past. The stains formed a maroon tracery that held Brak's eye like some hideous spider-webbing.

Blood dripping down. *Human blood.*

Behind the altar, and likewise of newer stone, rose a statue ceiling-high.

The carved eyes taunted him. The carved mouth curled downward in incredible malevolence. The carved hands, frozen stone, still seemed to beat upon the thighs of the crossed stone legs.

Like a man driven, Brak whirled and raced back along the short passage. His mind reeled.

He had remembered.

There was another image, dimly visible in a niche. He had glimpsed it without really seeing it during the march down to the confrontation with Tamar Zed. He was sure of it now. He'd seen a smaller version of the idol that

118

watched with lustful glee over the blooded altar.

Were there similar idols elsewhere in this damned house? New idols, their worship instituted simultaneously with the apparent possession of a model girl named Nordica?

The bile of fear rose in his throat. He saw Elinor ahead, her face a blur. He swiped at his eyes.

How to tell her that the most evil power known to the world now ruled this place?

How to tell her that they were in the lair of followers of Yob-Haggoth?

In that moment Brak knew why the mysterious rockslide had diverted his path south. He knew why he had recognized some familiar, mocking highlight behind the surfaces of Nordica's jade eyes. He knew why he had been so readily chosen as a replacement for Prince Pemma.

Septegundus, Yob-Haggoth's minister upon earth, had said, *I will be there.* But perhaps he'd left Brak's punishment to his daughter.

Brak's mind churned and fumed with vast terrors. He reached Elinor. There was a desperate curiosity in her glance.

"What did you find in there, Brak?"

His bowels twisted. He forced out words.

"Nothing. 'Tis just some storehouse or other. Not worth bothering about."

She started past him. "May I see—?"

He seized her forearm. "There's no time." And he thrust her down the passage which they'd been following.

Elinor's glance said full well that she knew something was wrong. But perhaps she had seen too much horror already to inquire after more. Brak was glad when they passed out of range of the glow from the cross-corridor. His mind hammered with doubts, fears, questions—

Was it Ariane, daughter of Septegundus, who had possessed Nordica?

If so, why was she so bent on performing the ritual and acquiring alchemical wealth. He could not fathom it.

Perhaps Ariane was involved in some scheme entirely separate from revenging herself against him, but his presence in the mountains had made it advantageous for

119

her to divert the course of his journey and gain two ends at once. He comprehended now Tamar Zed's veiled remarks about Nordica's power, as well as the Magian's apparent willingness to be humiliated by the witch-woman.

No man who had sold his being to Yob-Haggoth could do anything but grovel before the daughter of the god's Amyr upon Earth.

With extreme effort he forced the terrors from his mind and brought his attention back to the dark corridor through which he and Elinor were advancing at a slow pace.

He saw another yellow glow ahead. He darted well out in front of the girl once more, wondering fearfully what he would see when he glanced down this cross-passage.

It turned out to be a less forbidding sight. He spun back with a finger of caution to his mouth, realizing too late that Elinor had come up close behind. His shoulder struck hers. She cried out.

Brak tried to draw back from the right-angle intersection of the two passages. A short way down the right-hand corridor, a helmeted guard had been leaning on his spear, drowsing. His eyes popped open the moment Elinor made her outcry.

Dropping to one knee, Brak pulled the girl's head against his shoulder. He kept his own head down so that their faces would not shine in the reflection of the guard's niche lamp.

"Who is it? Who walks there?" The guard hefted his spear. Though he sounded somewhat hesitant, he advanced down the passage.

"Answer, whoever it is!"

Desperately Brak flogged his tired brain for a way out of this new dilemma. Beneath his knee he felt loose pebbles. Quickly he scooped up a handful, tossed them off in the dark. At the same time he let out a high-pitched squeaking cry.

The weird noise bounced from the echoing walls. The guard started, peered into the gloom. Brak hoped that the ticking of the tiny stones as they fell, coupled with the faint cry, would convince the guard that only fat gray rats ran in the darkness.

120

The guard hesitated in mid-stride.

Elinor's cheek was cold against Brak's side. He scooped up more pebbles, tossed them. The tick-ticking sound was softer this time. So was Brak's cry. He muffled it behind his hand.

The guard's shoulders slumped with relief.

"More of those filthy four-legged things—"

Muttering, he faced around. He returned to his post near the lamp niche and resumed leaning on his spear.

Breath whistled out between Brak's lips. Once more they had been spared. But how many more times could he bring it off before weariness and fear overcame him, addled his brains, slowed his reactions to the fatal point? Especially now that he knew Yob-Haggoth ruled this place?

When the guard began to doze again, Brak and the girl darted across the open intersection. They soon left the light behind.

Once more the passage sloped steeply upward. But the air seemed a trifle fresher, less tainted with the blood-musty aroma of the deep underground.

Distantly Brak heard shouting. He stopped to listen.

"Either my brain has cracked, girl, or that's the clamor of an army in battle."

Elinor was quick to agree: "You're right. I hear men yelling."

The barbarian pointed. "Look ahead. That grayness. A window? The noise comes from that direction."

They hurried on. The oblong of light did indeed turn out to be a tall, narrow embrasure. Pearly mist drifted through the opening in the wall, congealing in cold droplets on Brak's skin as he leaned across the sill in an effort to see out.

It seemed to be near dawn. But the night mist still whirled and gusted. Brak had a sense of being high above the battle scene, for the shoutings and armor-clashing occasionally grew faint. Once he glimpsed a yellowish flare, as of massed torches.

And after several more moments of careful listening, he identified the rattle of swords, the neigh of horses, the creak of wooden equipment wagons.

Joyfully he whirled back from the window.

121

"That's an army out there, right enough. Small—there aren't many fighting men left in the kingdom. But an army."

As Elinor's eyes glowed with fresh hope, the sweet, sharp notes of a military trumpet drifted through the gray dawn. Elinor caught her breath.

"Is it Prince Pemma? Or Lord Strann?"

"I expect so. And they've brought men to storm the walls. Can you hear that rumbling? Siege machines, I'll wager. We must free the other prisoners at once. With an attack going on, Nordica's soldiers are occupied. It's our best chance to escape. Hurry!"

The big man turned and raced up the corridor, battle fury stirring him. Elinor darted close behind.

Even as he ran, Brak heard a new sound—the heavy crashing of siege boulders striking the walls.

Around a bending in the corridor, light glimmered again.

"We're near the dungeon, I think," he growled.

He hurried on. So eager was he to use the outside attack to good advantage, that he failed to see the shadow of the approaching soldier.

The guard hove into sight around the bend, running. He carried a signal bugle. Elinor screamed.

The men saw one another simultaneously. The guard dropped the bugle, snaked his broadsword from its scabbard, charged Brak to run him through. Even as he attacked, he opened his mouth to shout an alarm.

With a long leap Brak dived against him, stifling the shout. The barbarian's thick fingers closed on the man's windpipe. He felt the broadsword whip past his ribs, nearly opening his side.

The guard flailed, struggled to bring his sword hand into position to chop at Brak's skull. By that time the big barbarian had closed all ten fingers on the soldier's scrawny neck to throttle him.

Here at last was an enemy of solid flesh. Rivers of primeval fury raced wild inside Brak then.

The guard struck for Brak's head with his sword. The blade clanged against the wall. Brak blinked in a shower of blue sparks, dodged the next hack, then hurled the guard against the wall with all his power.

The man's helmet tipped off his head, went rolling away down the sharply-pitched floor. Growling, Brak jerked the guard away from the wall, then smashed him against it again, just as the guard's sword came arcing toward Brak's muscle-thick neck.

Hands back on the soldier's windpipe, the barbarian crashed the man's skull against the stone an instant before the sword reached his throat. The angle of the blow changed as the back of the guard's head cracked open against the rock.

Eyes huge, horror-filled, the guard went limp. His sword fell out of his hand. Brak stepped away, panting. The guard toppled over.

Laughing low, Brak gave the corpse a kick. It spun over and over down the sloping corridor until it bumped against the wall at a bend. There it thumped to a standstill, the back of the head a grisly ruin of brains and oozing blood.

Brak seized the fallen broadsword. The touch of cold iron against his palm lent him new strength. He turned to signal for Elinor to follow.

With something akin to amusement, he saw that she was now as frightened of him as she was of anything. In truth Brak's face had turned ugly, as it did when the battle-heat sang and bubbled in his blood.

"Don't shudder so, girl," he said. "The only ones I'll kill are those who serve Ar—the witch-woman. Let's hurry. Time's running fast."

The barbarian and the girl raced along toward the light ahead. They emerged into the dungeon corridor, finding it deserted.

The boots of running men hammered in the distance. This sound was counterpointed by crashes and tremors which told that Prince Pemma or Lord Strann had siege engines strong enough to shake the castle walls.

Elinor pointed down the row of barred doorways. "It was that cell."

Brak hurried to the jailer's post at the end of the short lamplit corridor. He pulled a set of bronze keys from a peg. In the clamor of the sudden attack, all posts had been deserted, it seemed.

Brak ran along the cell doors shouting. "Darios? Runga?"

The smith's coarse voice responded. "This door! This one!"

Quickly Brak inserted the key, twisted it. He rushed inside.

"We have a chance to escape. Lord Strann is attacking the gates. We must—*what's wrong with the seaman?*"

Darios was lying on a straw pallet. His cheeks were chalk-colored, except for twin spots of red in their centers. His eyes shone glassy-bright.

Brak leaned down, felt the sailor's brow. The leathery skin burned against his palm.

"Fever, all right," Runga grunted. "Took sick hours ago."

Darios's lips opened. He strained upward, as if in recognition of Brak:

"The smith—during the night the smith was taken—"

Runga kicked the prone man's shoulder. "Taken nowhere, you salt-logged fool. 'Tis only your fever-dreams talking."

Hastily the smith turned toward an angry Brak.

"I didn't mean to strike him that way, barbarian. My temper's short, and the poor wretch has been moaning and seeing imps in every corner since the fever seized him. Let's leave him behind."

Feebly Darios's right hand lifted.

"Beware the smith. He was—he was—"

Darios shuddered and rolled onto his side, shaking violently. His speech became a babble.

Brak sorted through the collection of keys, found one which seemed the correct size. He inserted the key in Darios' wrist cuff. As he unlocked the shackle he glanced up at Runga.

"We won't leave him here or anywhere, smith. He was a prisoner exactly as we were."

Sensing the possibility of escape, Runga seemed to become unusually agreeable: "Very well, very well. Though you're assuming authority again, I won't quarrel. Take him along if you want. But his shouting and his ranting will bring the guards on the run, mark my word."

124

Brak hoisted the sick man to his feet. "Nevertheless, he goes with us."

Runga snatched the ring of keys and quickly unlocked his own iron bonds. Then the smith hurried out of the cell. Brak led Darios into the corridor. The seaman's wood leg rasped on the stone.

"Help me carry him," Brak said to Runga.

Grudgingly the smith took up his part of the burden. His eyes were oddly bright as he peered at Brak a moment. Was the smith also taking ill?

The big barbarian kept his right hand free, the dead soldier's broadsword ready, as they set out up the tunnel. Darios continued to mutter and mumble. His lips shone with fever-spittle.

The passage turned, then branched. The left branching ran parallel to the castle wall. Down that way Brak saw an oak door standing open. Beyond the door was a parapet jammed with soldiers, cursing, discharging crossbows, hurling spears. Iron arrow-bolts flicked over the rampart from below.

"That way is useless," Brak whispered to the smith. "Take the right turning."

In another moment they were hurrying along a passage where torches hung in brackets at regular intervals. Brak called to Elinor:

"Snatch down one of those, girl. It'll help light our way."

By now Brak had no notion of where they were heading; he was unfamiliar with the plan of the upper part of the castle. But at least flight was preferable to an encounter with Nordica's men. Perhaps they could still find a way out.

Darios stumbled along, moaning. His speech grew coherent a moment: "Beware the smith. He was taken—"

Taken, taken, taken, taken—

With no advance warning, the echo of the reedy voice sprang back upon the hurrying quartet from all directions. Cold, moist air washed against Brak's skin. He halted.

The echo rose up and rang through what sounded like a vast space. By extending his hand Brak discovered that the corridor walls had vanished. They were in another hall

125

or cavern within the palace.

The stifling air began to choke out the torch Elinor was carrying. Turgid black smoke drifted from the end of the brand. Brak was ready to turn back when, high overhead, he heard a rustling, a sinister flapping.

Soft at first. Then louder. As of many wings being unfurled.

Brak seized the torch, thrust it high over his head. Light sparkled off hundreds of tiny scarlet gems. But these gems were in motion, points of brilliance that swooped and darted. The flapping grew louder.

"We've roused a den of bats," Brak yelled. "Go back the way we came——"

Dry wings, heavily veined, struck him in the face.

Brak let go of Darios, reeled back as the bat swooped down on his forearm. Runga shrieked, turned to flee.

The grayish-white bat had wings nearly as wide as the reach of Brak's outstretched arms. It bumped against his forearm below the elbow. Suddenly Brak threw back his head, rigid with agony.

Through his whole body burned an agonizing pain worse than any he had ever suffered.

He wrenched his arm, tried to shake the bat away. Choking in horror and pain, he saw that the bat-creature had small, semi-transparent sacs where its claws should be. Into these sacs pressed against Brak's skin, darkish fluid was draining.

His blood——

All around, a cloud of bats flapped and swooped. One fastened on Elinor's cheek. She tore at its throat, ripped the sacs loose. Each sac had a small sucking mouth on the bottom. Blood-bats. Blood-bats out of hell, draining human blood and human life——

Wrenching, flailing, Brak tried to dislodge the bat from his arm. It hung on with grisly tenacity, the sacs already a quarter filled with blood. How that blood passed through unbroken skin. Brak did not know or care, tormented as he was by the excruciating agony of the contact.

The broadsword slipped from his limp fingers. Bats by the dozen whirled and skated through the air around the huddled group of humans, each bat hunting a place to strike.

126

One settled on the forehead of Darios. Brak seized the torch from Elinor's hand, thrust its tattered flame against the bloated bat's obscenely small head.

The blood-bat on Darios's forehead gave out a high-pitched, keening sound as the tongues of fire ate half its head away. Suddenly its sucking sacs unfastened.

Brak trampled on the filthy thing as it fell to the cavern floor, sacs oozing droplets of red. On his own bare arm he saw a row of purple indentations, deep and bloodshot, left by the bat that had released the moment Brak brought the torch over toward Darios.

Another bat was attacking Elinor. Brak burned its right wing in the fire.

The bat flapped loose, went soaring away into the high black, uttering that tormented keening sound.

Elinor was on her knees. She used her bare hands in a futile struggle with another of the gray-white things that darted at her face. The tiny sucking-mouth sacs nearly touched her flesh— .

Howling, Brak grasped the torch in both hands like a sword and began to sweep the air with it. Back and forth, back and forth, the torch trailed fire and sparks. The tiniest of those sparks was enough to send the blood-bats flying.

Brak and Elinor stood back to back in the center of a ring of torchlight while the ghastly flapping and rustling went on, just out of reach of the barbarian's sputtering brand.

"Help him up," Brak panted to Elinor, indicating Darios.

The girl tried to lift the mariner by the shoulders. Darios was limp, exhausted. His eyes were marble-shiny. He comprehended that the girl was trying to help him, struggled erect.

"Pick up my sword," Brak told the girl. "With the fire we may have a chance to get out of here. Runga can carry Dar—Where is Runga?"

"Ran—away," Elinor gasped. "Ran the first moment those—things attacked."

Before Brak could even spew out a curse, he heard a new sound.

Many men.

Running.

Momentarily another sound was added—the bawl of a familiar voice:

"This way, soldiers! In the cavern. I told Nordica I'd serve her well and now I've done so. I've led you to the escaped prisoners. Someone pass me a torch."

Suddenly one entire wall of the cavern seemed to blaze with fire. Brak stared in stunned rage as a band of Nordica's men swarmed through the entrance. Each man carried a lighted brand.

And there among the soldiers was Runga.

Laughing, the smith held his own light high overhead to fend off the blood-bats. With so many torches present, the creatures now went sailing back up to their perches in the shadows of the chamber's roof.

Grotesque shadows twisted over the rock floor as Brak dropped the torch, snatched the broadsword from Elinor, lunged.

He heard Darios' cry:

"Beware the smith! I tried to warn you he was taken—"

"Seize them!" Runga shouted at the soldiers. "Then go tell Nordica Fire-Hair who ran to summon you."

Runga's voice died in the thudding of boots, the oaths of the fighting men who were swarming around the big barbarian. Brak stabbed at one guard's neck, missed. Hands seized his sword arm and sword wrist. The weapon was wrenched away.

Sword hilts and spear butts crashed against his head. Bloodied, wrathful, he struck out with his hammer-like fists.

But there were too many soldiers. Brak went to his knees.

Moments later, hovering on the edge of consciousness, he was lifted by four soldiers and borne from the catacomb.

Nordica's men dragged Darios and Elinor along. Shortly the party emerged in the open air of the castle courtyard. Brak was set groggily on his feet. A short distance away, Brak saw Runga, arms folded, laughing.

There was no man guarding the smith, or even holding him fast.

Chapter X

THE GATES OF SORCERY

Brak's eyes slitted down as the guards manhandled him to a stop in the high-walled courtyard. The wind sent gritty particles of dust against his eyelids. That wind whined, blowing, it seemed, first from one direction, then another.

Hanging between his two guards while the other soldiers formed a circle around him, Brak stared at the peaks of the mountains visible above the ramparts. Clouds of morning mist scudded past the summits. From the movement of the clouds, he judged that the wind was blowing gustily, and with mounting force. And even though the wind scattered much of the low-lying ground mist, the morning still seemed dim, like a sinister pall.

"The winds are rising," Brak said to himself. "She said they would."

Elinor, also held by two of Nordica's burly men, heard his muttered words. She glanced at him apprehensively. "It's the time of the seasonal storms. Hardly a living creature dares keep to the upper slopes when those winds blow."

"So she said."

"Nordica?"

"Aye, girl. She told me—" A shudder of uncertainty. *Who really hid behind the witch-girl's jade eyes?* "—She told me she'd perform the ritual when the winds rose. Take our bodies and—"

He bit off the sentence, seeing that he had alarmed her. To the armor-clad commander of the guards he said:

"Where is she, soldier? Let's get this finished."

The commander fetched Brak a hard blow across the jaw. The big barbarian was thrown backward in the grip

130

of his captors. His mouth opened in a wild bellow of rage. Recovering, he lunged forward. A spear-point pricked his naked backbone.

"My man behind you," said the commander, "would as lief gut you as not, outlander. But I want to deliver you to Lady Nordica. Our friend the smith"—he indicated the smirking Runga—"did us a service by calling our attention to your escape. For your own sake, don't move. And speak only when someone addresses you."

Brak bit his lip. His body ached. Several of his wounds bled. He tried to concentrate on his surroundings, on the courtyard, as the guard commander strode toward a figure almost invisible in the shadows near the high, barred gates.

High on the mountain, a wild bird flew out of a mist-cloud, its wings beating frantically, as if it fled from some supernatural force. Brak's spine crawled. He realized that he could hear the wind's whine because the clatter of swords and the grind of siege engines outside the walls had stopped.

Nowhere did Brak spy Nordica, though her troops lined the parapets that overlooked the road leading up to the castle. The commander reached the gate, joined the shadowy figure that seemed to be bent over studying something. At the commander's arrival, the shadowman straightened up. Half his face turned into the light.

It was Tamar Zed.

The Magian's robes whipped in the wind. He had been peering through a spy-hole cut in the heavy timbers of the gate. What was he watching outside? The army's preparation for a new attack?

The guard commander pointed to Brak, Elinor and Darios. The seaman lay sprawled on the ground, mumbling feverishly. Tamar threw Brak one long, hateful glance. Then he turned back to his spy port, more interested for the moment in events outside.

Ignoring the commander's warning, Brak spoke to a soldier in the group guarding the prisoners:

"What happened to Prince Pemma's troops? Have they retreated?"

The soldier snickered. "You might say that."

"You mean they're no longer besieging the castle?"

"Who knows what they're doing, except standing still as sheep?"

"But why would they stop—?"

"Didn't the commander tell you to keep silent, lout?"

Brak glared, turned away.

He glanced at Runga. The smith was sauntering toward the prisoners. As he approached, Brak's hands itched for a broadsword. He imagined the pleasure of lopping the arrogant head from the thick shoulders.

Runga shoved past the guards, stood before Brak with fists on hips.

"Well, outlander. Who has the authority now, eh?"

The smile left Runga's lips suddenly. He lashed out with his forearm, striking Brak's jaw, snapping his head back.

Like a great tree Brak stood his ground, shaking from the blow but not falling.

"And to think she fancied you for a lover!" Runga jeered. "A brute! Uncivilized, ignorant! She found a better man in me, I'll warrant. I promised I'd repay her favors. I kept my word."

"You simpleton! You gave yourself to—"

"To bliss a fool like you can't imagine," Runga cut in. "Yes, I was summoned. After you and the whimpering shepherd girl were disposed of, she found out. She was angry with the Magian. So she"—a lewd smile—"diverted herself with other pleasures. What happened in her chambers is beyond belief. The kind of experience a man dreams about but never—"

Runga stopped. His brow was suddenly beaded with perspiration. He gripped Brak's arm. The barbarian would have thrown off the clammy fingers, except for the intense light in Runga's eyes. It told Brak that the smith was owned now, possessed.

Not by a woman.

By the Dark One. Yob-Haggoth.

Runga's voice grew hoarse:

"You have no idea what kind of person she is, outlander."

"But I do," Brak breathed.

Runga seemed not to hear. "She is not as she appears."

Remembering the treacherous beauty of Ariane, he said, "I know."

The smith started. "You know? How is that possible?"

"Never mind." He stared into Runga's eyes. Deep in them he saw stark fear. "I hope you burn, smith. I think you will. I know what you had to do to gain what you wanted. I too have encountered Yob-Haggoth."

At this Runga's face wrenched. He made the sign against the evil eye. Abruptly his arrogant manner vanished. He licked at slack lips.

"I had to betray you," Runga whined. "To be summoned by her once—to be allowed to touch her—to know all the arts she can call upon to make a man's guts boil—and then to be ordered away with never another chance unless your loyalty's proved. I—I had to do it."

"Yes," was the bleak reply. "She tried to tempt me once too."

Runga's eyebrows raised. "Nordica?"

"Not Nordica. The—other."

And then Runga realized that Brak truly knew everything.

Puzzled by much of the exchange, Elinor still grasped the essence of it. "May the gods curse you, smith."

When Runga laughed, it was not a sound of triumph or joy. It was a sound of heartbreak.

"They already have," he said.

He turned his back and walked off, trying to swagger. He made a poor job of it.

Brak looked down at the aged mariner. Darios gazed unseeing at the wind-haunted, mist-torn skies. To Elinor, Brak said:

"He tried to warn us. He kept chattering about Runga being taken somewhere. I wish we had understood what he meant."

Forlorn, Elinor nodded.

Silence then. The wind moaned. Awful images of Yob-Haggoth flitted in Brak's brain like the tag ends of nightmare.

He looked at the guards. Confident of their ability to confine the prisoners with little effort, they had all turned to face the high, barred gates where Tamar Zed still crouched before the spy-hole. The men appeared to be awaiting a signal, or some news of what transpired outside. Surely the army Prince Pemma had brought was regrouping for a new assault. Nothing else could explain the unnatural quiet.

Brak studied the gates. A mammoth oaken log lay in L-shaped prongs, holding them shut. He frowned. A plan, risky yet feasible, suggested itself.

The big barbarian glanced back at the jumbled towers and battlements of the castle proper. He hoped that Nordica—odd, how he kept thinking of her by that name—would not soon be finished with whatever hell's work was keeping her closeted inside.

He listened. He hoped for a sound—chariot-chains, siege-engine wheels—to tell him that Pemma's force was preparing to move forward again.

But he heard nothing.

Nor could he tell much from the postures of Nordica's men on the ramparts. They stood like so many statues, crossbows and spears ready, their attention centered on the roadway outside.

Brak wiped an ooze of blood from his left side. He drew a deep breath. He cupped his hands around his mouth and called:

"Magian?"

At the gateway, Tamar Zed spun from the spy-hole.

"Magian, listen! I have an amusing joke to tell you!"

Tamar Zed's bearded face stood out in lines of hatred as the guard commander started running toward Brak to silence him. The soldiers crowded in close, swords ready.

"Keep him silent!" Tamar shouted to the hurrying commander. "There must be no commotion to disturb events outside."

"The commotion," Brak shouted back, "was already here, inside, Magian. Quite a lusty commotion, too. Do you recognize this sign?"

And, with a coarse laugh, Brak suddenly extended the index and the last fingers of his right hand, both middle fingers bent down to form the horn-symbol.

Tamar went white.

After a moment the Magian gathered his robes around him, staring in fury and confusion at the big barbarian.

134

Brak towered in the rising wind, great right arm outstretched. At its end, the cuckold-horns formed by his fingers shook, mockingly.

"Wear these, Magian," Brak cried. "They fit you now."

And he jammed the back of his hand against his forehead, putting the horns on himself, jeeringly.

The guard commander broke through the circle of men, tore a spear from the hands of one, aimed it at Brak.

"Stupid lout! I warned you to keep silent!"

"*Hold!*"

The captain's head whipped around. Brak kept the horns against his forehead.

Tamar Zed had called the order to stop.

The Magian came running, white-cheeked. He passed Runga, whose baffled expression was just shading into understanding. The smith took a step forward. All at once he saw the commander signal, saw one of the soldiers hoist his spear back over his shoulder, its point aimed at Runga's middle. The smith froze.

Tamar rushed up to Brak.

The Magian's black eyes burned fire-bright as he lashed out with his right hand. He knocked Brak's horn-fingers aside.

Brak let his arm drop without protest. But he laughed.

"Be careful, barbarian," Tamar said. "Nordica wants you alive. But I have something to say about that, too."

"You have nothing to say about that. She owns you."

" 'Ware how you speak in front of these men!" Tamar spat sibilantly.

"They'll know the truth soon enough. They'll know who she really is."

Tamar Zed swallowed. "Do—you know?"

"Yes."

"What else—?"

"That she caused me to come into this land by arranging a rockslide so I could take but one road."

The words made Tamar's eyes flicker briefly with amusement. Apparently that part was no secret to Nordica's henchman. But the Magian's mind quickly reverted to the original topic. Because some of the soldiers had heard Brak's taunts and were staring at the two with open

135

curiosity, Tamar was moved to stress his authority as best he could:

"I can easily have something to say about what happens to you, outlander. For example, I can provide Lady Nordica with a ready explanation of an unfortunate accident. You attempted to escape. These men and their worthy commander were forced to slay you. How you came back from the tunnel down which I sent you and the girl I can't say, but——"

"She almost roasted you for that one, I hear," the big barbarian chuckled.

The shaft hit home. Sweating, Tamar forced bravado.

"I still have authority to send you on a far darker journey. To death. I'll do it if you continue to mock me with the filthy joke of those horns."

"Call it a joke if you like, Magian. You have no choice but to wear them."

"You're lying," Tamar whispered. His hand tore the enameled dagger from the scabbard at his waist. "You'd never dare admit such a thing. You know what I did when I caught the two of you together. I'd do it again if I learned that you and she——"

"How can you do anything?" Brak jeered. "She's your ruler, she and her father——"

Another direct hit. Tamar Zed blanched.

"—and the master they serve." Brak's eyes slid past Tamar Zed's face to the staring guards. His voice dropped to a guttural. "Do I need to repeat aloud the name of that master to prove that I know?"

A ferocious tic beat in Tamar's cheek. His voice was weak. "The—one of whom you speak—his servitors —they are not my rulers in everything——"

"You're lying."

"They are not my rulers!" Tamar shrieked, and drove the point of the knife at Brak's throat.

But something stayed the Magian's hand at the last second. He only touched the barbarian's neck hard enough to bring a glistening dollop of blood to the surface. Elinor cried out softly.

"You're frightened, barbarian," Tamar panted, as though saying it could make it true. "Frightened and

136

trying to strike back at me. You couldn't have been with Nordica. You were in the tunnel all the time. You got out somehow and now you're trying to anger me with your mockery. That's it, isn't it? Admit it!"

Everything, including Brak's very life, hung in precarious balance now. The point of the dagger dug the flesh of his neck. But he moved anyway.

With one lightning motion he brought his forearm up and under the dagger, leaping back. So swift and powerful was the blow, the soldiers barely had time to react. Brak grabbed Tamar's outstretched wrist, twisted it till the Magian's dagger pointed straight at Runga.

"Look, you stargazing fool!" he shouted. "There's the one who mocks you. Ask *him* about the delights Nordica offered. Ask *him* who summoned him at a time when Nordica didn't care to have *you* around."

Tamar Zed's lip began to tremble. For the first time, he seemed frail, weak, craven.

"Not true," he said. "She'd never—"

"*Ask him!*"

Slowly Tamar Zed turned to stare at Runga.

The smith tried to bluff with a sneer. Tamar Zed's lips compressed, almost bloodless. His stare was vicious and piercing.

Man for man, Tamar was the more imposing. His position as a Magian contributed to this, doubtless. In any event, Runga's defenses slipped. A nervous flicker of his eyelids, plus his unwillingness to look at Tamar Zed directly, gave him away.

Tamar faced Brak again. "Now I know the one to punish."

No longer craven, Tamar was lean and terrible in his fury. He walked toward Runga, who tried to flee, but a second too late.

Tamar Zed's dagger whipped up, arced down. Runga screamed, threw up his arms to fend the blow, screamed in fear.

Because of his awkward posture, Runga's feet tangled. He fell. As he did, Tamar Zed buried the blade in his arm.

Blood spurted. The soldiers around Brak gasped. Tamar tore the dagger from Runga's flesh, trying to remedy the failure of his first blow by striking another,

137

fatal one. In that instant, when all heads were turned to watch the struggle, Brak lunged.

His hands closed on a guard's bony wrist, constricted. The man let go of his broadsword, shrieking. His wrist bones cracked, pulped by Brak's mighty squeeze. Brak seized the fallen sword.

"On the ground, girl!" he shouted, giving Elinor a shove that sprawled her alongside the semiconscious Darios. Then he laughed. This time the laugh was bold.

Laughing louder, a battle roar, Brak began to hew his way out of the circle of confused soldiers.

A spear-head flashed for his throat. Brak's sword-swing hacked the spear in half. The tip of his blade ripped in and out of the soldier's left eyesocket. The man tumbled back, spilling into two more guards.

A path out of the ring lay open. But first the barbarian finished his swing, turning full circle with his blade extended at arm's length.

Soldiers leaped back to avoid that scythe of death. Two failed to save themselves. As they dropped, Brak went jumping over the convulsing bodies of three other fallen men. He raced for the barred gates.

The soldiers on the battlements spotted his flight. The air began to whine and buzz, full of iron darts from crossbows. Brak dodged, ran in an erratic line. He halved the distance to the gate. Quartered it.

Runga was attempting to rise and run. He was making a bad job of it because of his arm wound. Then, like a sudden apparition, Tamar Zed was in Brak's path, dagger poised.

The Magian charged, mystically-silvered robes flying on the rising wind. Brak thrust out with his broadsword. Tamar dodged aside, drove the dagger in toward Brak's face.

The point raked a long, pain-hot furrow from the front of Brak's cheekbone to his right ear. Tamar Zed's lunge carried him on unchecked. Brak brought his sword up from below.

"Let Yob-Haggoth repair you if he can," Brak howled, and rammed the killing iron into the Magian's bowels.

Tamar Zed shrieked and spun away, dying.

138

Brak ran on. He was bleeding heavily from the cheek wound, as well as from another gash opened in his shoulder by a grazing crossbow bolt. But he was under the shadow of the battlements now—nearly to the gate where only the heavy oaken crossbar stood between him and Prince Pemma's army.

Running at top speed, Brak crashed into the gate. He thrust his left shoulder beneath the oak bar at the place where the two gates met. He crouched down, lifted—

The great bar was ponderously heavy. Brak had only raised it halfway to the top of the L-prongs when the remainder of the guard party charged.

A spear flashed past his face, buried in the right-hand door. The weight on Brak's shoulders was excruciating. His whole body cried out in torment as he lifted, lifted, at the same time slashing back and forth with the sword in his extended right hand.

The guard commander darted in under the cover of the long spears held by his men. Brak tried to parry the commander's blade, missed. The commander's mouth twisted into a triumphant grin.

Time seemed to stop there in the murky, wind-haunted courtyard. Brak saw the commander's broadsword thrusting silvery-swift for his throat. He felt the agonizing weight of the bar begin to buckle his straining legs.

The great bar came free of the prongs. Brak's pull dragged it away from the gate with sudden violence. Brak threw himself backward to keep from being crushed. The commander's sword buried in the free-swinging end of the beam. The bar dropped. There was an inhuman cry of pain—

The guard commander lay on the ground, broken in half, his midsection an ooze beneath the reddened beam.

Wildly Brak tugged at a black iron ring, hauled the left-hand door open, slipped through.

"Pemma! Prince Pemma!"

Brak screamed it, breaking from the open gate, brandishing his sword, a grisly figure. His bronzed skin and lion pelt streamed with blood. His yellow braid flew as he bolted down the slope.

"Prince! Order your troops through the gate, Prince! Now, before—"

140

He skidded to a halt on the shaly earth that sloped away from the castle wall. The echo of his voice died away. A snarling filled the silence. Utter horror and fear swept over Brak.

Nordica Fire-Hair was not hiding within the castle. She stood a few paces ahead. Her jade eyes first showed surprise, then amusement.

"I know you, Ariane!" Brak screamed.

"That makes no difference now, Brak," she laughed.

Nordica's fiery hair danced in the wind, as did the hem of her gown. Around her left wrist coiled a light chain of silver links. At the other end of the chain a silver collar circled the gray throat of Scarletjaw.

The great hound stirred, rising on its forelegs to swing its monstrous head and glare at Brak with murderous eyes.

Then Brak saw the worst.

Beyond Nordica on the lower slope, Prince Pemma sat a war pony. Near him, on an open litter, lay his father, Strann. Behind them were several hundred ragtag soldiers, heavily armed, and siege equipment, and baggage wagons.

Not a man raised a weapon to help him. Brak knew the day was lost.

The silence outside the castle walls had been the silence of an army cowed, an army held at bay, an army bewitched—

Bewitched by one slim girl and the great evil dog at the end of the silver chain.

Chapter XI

BLOW, HELL-WINDS!

In Brak's brain that instant, the entire scene imprinted itself for all time. The dark day. The mountains, sharp-craggy and savage, only partially visible behind the blowing mist. And the winds.

The winds seemed to swirl from one quarter of the sky, then from another. They roused clouds of dust on every hand.

At first Brak couldn't believe the evidence of his own senses. Then, as he looked at the assembled soldiers, saw their fear and apathy, his mind recognized the truth.

He felt the whip and sting of dust against both cheeks. *The wind came from two directions at once.*

With conscious effort he focused his attention on Nordica. She stood silent, haughty, gazing back at him across her shoulder. In the gloominess of the day, her eyes shone with sparkling green lights.

Suddenly her body seemed to shimmer and fade. He saw another woman in her place. A woman of beauty even more incredible than Nordica's.

A lushly curved body was outlined by tight-clinging, midnight-colored silks. The eyes were dark as the starless winter sky. Black hair floated like a cloud. She smiled with lascivious, plum-colored lips—

Ariane of Hell. Exactly as he remembered her from the Ice-marches. Beautiful enough to tempt a man beyond all reason, as she had tempted him. But he had rebuffed her. Refused her promise of he wealth of all the kingdoms of the world in return for fealty to her and to the obscene god she served.

There she was, shimmering in the air behind the illusory presence of Nordica. Did the soldiers see her? He doubted it. This was probably more of her witch-working, for his benefit alone. She wanted him to see the expression in her eyes—

An immortal, consuming hatred.

The illusion wavered. The very air blurred, melted. Nordica was there once more. But the eyes were still the eyes of Ariane.

Brak struggled to bring sound from his throat. "Prince Pemma? Order your troops forward. Order them to attack."

The young prince's war pony danced and snorted. Its eyes rolled frantically as it shied away from Scarletjaw. The hound's tongue lolled out red and slimy between its long fangs.

Behind him, Brak heard a jingle of trappings. It was

142

already too late. Nordica's men were slipping out through the open gates.

Nordica whirled around. "Back! And leave the gates standing wide. Let's see whether the barbarian can rouse these men to strike at me."

The castle soldiers retreated into the courtyard.

Still Nordica continued to watch Brak, amused. He took a tighter grip on his sword, walked wide of Scarletjaw as the hound rose on his haunches. The putrescent smell rising from the dog's gray hide-plates nearly made the barbarian retch.

He passed Nordica, avoiding those lustfully cruel eyes, and approached Pemma and Strann.

The Lord of the Silver Balances looked pale in his dress armor. He supported himself on the litter cushions with his elbow.

Brak decided to bluff. He swung his blade in a wide arc to indicate the troops. "What's the matter with them? The gate is open. Surely one woman cannot stop you. Nor even that four-legged thing. Scarletjaw cannot stop an army!"

Rank upon rank, the men loyal to Strann's standard stood immobile. They eyed Brak with open hostility.

Brak knew one of the reasons they were stricken so. Even if they did not realize Nordica's identity—more properly, the identity of the witch-creature who had seized Nordica's body and mind for perverted ends—they recognized the menace of awful magical power. Brak realized he had but one hope left. Perhaps if the soldiers understood the truth about Nordica—

Before Pemma could reply to his challenge, Strann leaned forward on the litter.

"You don't know the things she's been saying to them, Brak. The things she's promised them."

He could imagine. He dissembled, replying, "Loot? Power? She'll take it all for herself, regardless of what she promises now. I know that because I know who she really is."

Both Lord Strann and Prince Pemma seemed too bemused to grasp the significance of that last sentence. Heart thudding inside his huge chest, Brak stalked around Pemma's pony to the front rank of soldiers. He confronted an officer who was leaning on his sword.

143

"Doesn't the loyalty you bear to Lord Strann mean anything to you? Will you forget it so easily?"

The officer scowled. "Stand aside, outlander. *She* commands here."

Brak would have rammed his broadsword into the craven man's guts had he not seen similar expressions on dozens of faces round about: slack-lipped attention, glistening-eyed lust.

Cursing, Brak whirled and walked back toward Pemma. Time to try to swing the balance with the ultimate revelation. But before he could speak, Nordica raised her right hand for silence.

Brak whispered up to the prince on horseback: "What in the name of the gods has unmanned them?"

Pemma's helmet plume bobbed in the wind. "What first made them hold their fire was the fact that she's a woman. She came out alone, save for the dog. Then, by the time they remembered that she's more than a woman—the enemy—it was too late. What has unmanned them"—Pemma looked forlorn—"is greed."

The sweet, bell-tinkling voice of Nordica Fire-Hair drifted over Brak's shoulder:

"What I have promised you, soldiers, is not empty boasting. Not dreams. Reality. The old man lying yonder in the litter is weak, nigh to death. His power in this land is finished. It deserves to be. There is a new power rising. The power of the mightiest god in creation. I serve that god because he is a god who speaks to the hearts of men. He knows their innermost lusts and desires. He fulfills them! I serve the Dark One proudly. I serve immortal Yob-Haggoth!"

Exalted, Nordica threw her arms wide and stood rigid, a lustfully beatific expression heightening her unholy beauty. Here and there among the soldiers a man stirred or jostled his neighbor or actually trembled, hearing the name of the god revealed. But to most, the invocation of the name of the supreme evil brought little more than a blank stare.

The ignorant craned forward, full of attention, wanting to know how their allegiance to Nordica would benefit them personally. Brak was sickened at the sight of so much unconcealed avarice. As in a sick delirium, he heard Nordica continue:

"It doesn't matter whether you know the god I serve. Serve only me! Turn your backs on Lord Strann. He's a weakling. His blood line has run thin. Only I possess the secret of Celsus Hyrcanus. I took it into my hands for one express purpose. To create untold wealth. To create untold wealth that shall in turn create armies of untold might and power. And those armies shall create dominion for the Dark One to the ends of the earth."

At last Brak began to understand.

Septegundus had sent his daughter Ariane to invade Nordica's body in order that the alchemical secret might become the property of the minions of Yob-Haggoth. The implications staggered his mind.

With the ability to transmute base metals into gold, the Dark One's followers could indeed mount armies of unprecedented size. And that, in turn, could signal the coming of the long, dark night of sin and demon-rule of which the Nestorian Jerome had warned in the Ice-marches.

Nordica was shrieking above the wind now, her words like knives in Brak's brain:

"Take heed of the bargain I offer! Your choice is clear. Remain with Strann—a sick graybeard. Attack my castle and risk your lives against my men and my little pet—" On the silver leash Scarletjaw stirred, teeth dripping saliva. "Or follow me. Follow me because I possess the secret the mystics have sought for age upon age. Follow me and your wealth, your power, will know no limit. A small band of men no larger than the one I see here can form the nucleus of a mighty host to sweep from the Pillars of Ebon to the Mountains of Smoke—from the Ice-marches in the north to Khurdisan in the south—and claim it all!"

For Yob-Haggoth! Brak's mind screamed.

But his voice remained stilled.

Nordica's jade eyes seemed to reach out to every soldier's face, tempting, infernally bright. The barbarian's very brain ached, because he remembered once again how sorely he had been tempted by this same Ariane.

"Who will follow me?" she cried. "*Who will follow me and rule the world?*"

145

Lord Strann seemed to be gasping for breath. The wind whined in the silence. A soldier scuffed his boot.

From the back of the ranks a voice called, "How do we know you have the secret, woman?"

"She doesn't," someone else shouted. "It doesn't exist and never will."

A red-bearded soldier towering tall above the rest shook his fist. "I say take the risk! I've never heard of this god of hers, but if even a tenth of what she promises is true, we'll be rich as potentates. I say take the chance and to the pit with Lord Strann!"

Through the army rippled an undercurrent of agreement. Only here and there did an isolated man shake his head or bite his lips, recognizing somehow the insidiously sweet evil that lay in Nordica's words.

Strann tried to turn on his litter to face his soldiers. He accomplished the movement with an effort that turned him pale. But for a moment his voice rose clear, strong, impassioned:

"To betray me is to betray more than the office I hold. You'll betray the people of this kingdom—perhaps all kingdoms! My own people are trusting you to destroy this sinkhole of magic and murder. I have heard something of this god of hers. An abomination! Don't listen to her, I beg you. Take up your swords and spears and we'll drive her back into her house and down to hell where she belongs!"

Gasping, Strann fell back on the litter. Prince Pemma dismounted. He hurried to his father's side, knelt down. Anguish twisted his stocky peasant face.

Brak watched the soldiers. Strann's words had produced an outbreak of derisive hoots and laughter. Nordica sensed her advantage. She jerked on the silver chain.

Scarletjaw lunged to his feet. Soldiers in the front rows shrank back. Nordica laughed.

"Well?" she exclaimed. "Who do you follow? Me? Or the addle-witted old man? Let those who are cowards stand where they are. Let those who would ride with me tomorrow to conquer the kingdoms of the earth throw down their weapons, turn their backs and return to their homes tonight!"

The red-bearded mercenary bawled, "Count me as one!

I'm sick of risking my skin for a king not even strong enough to rise off his couch. I don't know this god of yours, but I'll go gladly!"

So saying, he cast his spear to the earth. He flung his broadsword after it. Then he turned and shouldered his way out through the rear ranks.

Many heads turned to watch. A soldier with an oafish face giggled, an eerie sound in the keening wind. He wiped drool from his slack lips. He tossed his helmet and weapons atop redbeard's, and followed him away.

"Wait!"

Brak's voice was thunder in the wind. Redbeard and the oafish one turned around.

"I know Yob-Haggoth," he shouted. "In my journeyings I encountered his followers. And I nearly became a human sacrifice on his altar. What this woman offers you is a poison promise. You all remember the sudden change that came over the daughter of the alchemist?"

Nods, grunts of assent.

"Some thought that Nordica Fire-Hair was possessed. Well, it's true. This woman is not Nordica. Nordica's body, yes, but there the resemblance ends. She's a witch. The foulest witch in creation. The daughter of the sorcerer men call the Amyr of Evil upon Earth. She seized Nordica's body, then brought her lackeys here—the Magian, that hell-hound too—because Yob-Haggoth needs the corruption of souls that wealth can buy. I don't know how this witch heard of Celsus and his alchemical secret, but she has far-seeing powers—"

Nordica's words were a hiss on the wind. "Beware, Brak!"

He spun on her, struck nearly blind by the coruscating lights in her eyes. He fought against dizziness, snarled back:

"I was dead the moment you discovered me on the road here, wasn't I, Ariane?".

"Long before that. My father warned you."

"And you saw an opportunity to avenge yourself while completing the other part of your plan to seize the alchemical secret on behalf of Yob-Haggoth—"

Abruptly he stopped, his face sweaty-cold. He whirled again.

148

During the exchange with Nordica he had lost the attention of the soldiers. Led by the sneering redbeard and his oafish companion, others in the small army were waving their fists at him. He heard filthy references to his barbaric looks and behavior.

Worst of all, many of the soldiers were laughing. They did not believe.

"I tell you she'll lead you to destruction!" he roared. "Listen to me. *Listen*—!"

Useless.

In bands of two or three, then in groups of five and ten, the soldiers began to cast their armor into great heaps and walk away down the road.

A few still jested softly. Most seemed to slink. When fully a dozen men in the front rank turned to hurry down the hillside, joining the trickle of men that was rapidly becoming a torrent, Brak could stand it no longer. He shrieked in red rage.

Scarletjaw leaped out to meet the barbarian's attack, fangs sharp and bright as the sword Brak drove toward Nordica's bosom.

Nordica gave a ferocious jerk to the silver chain. She spat a word Brak did not understand. At once the dog changed direction.

Scarletjaw loped for Strann's litter. Brak slowed down, seeing the trap an instant before Nordica sprang it by jerking the silver chain again.

The hound slid to a halt, immense claws digging the shale. The monster dog was only a short distance from Strann and his kneeling son.

"Strike me and my hand will slip the chain," Nordica breathed. "The first to die will be Strann. The second will be his son."

Brak's sword was a leaden thing in his right fist. His head began to throb again. His eyes watered. His mouth burned. And as though in a nightmare, he saw the flesh of Nordica Fire-Hair's face peel away.

Beneath it was the bone-white grin of a skull.

Brak flung an arm across his eyes. The skull melted. Huge as black suns, Ariane's lustful dark eyes loomed in his brain. Her hair floated soft around her, a drift of ebony serpents—

In agony he dropped his broadsword. He drove the palms of his hands against his eyesockets ferociously hard. He growled like a tormented beast.

The illusion passed. He raised his head, panting.

Nordica's jade eyes regarded him with cool confidence. She whispered:

"Let your reason, not your hate, direct you, Brak. For as much as I despise you because of—the past—I still need you."

Lightly Nordica gestured to the lowering sky. The racing mist-clouds rode the winds across the high summits.

"By nightfall, Brak, the seasonal winds will peak. I must summon their power for the ritual. Tonight I must make the first transmutation—the first of many—to increase the power of Yob-Haggoth a thousandfold. So give me your answer. Your life—or theirs."

Strann shouted weakly, "Don't listen, Brak! Slay her!"

Scarletjaw strained on the chain, digging the earth with his claws. Pemma looked unsure. He glanced at his father, then at Brak. Nordica's expression changed to one of impatience.

"Which is it, Brak? Shall I loose the beast? Or will you return with me and play your part?"

Black fears and red angers consumed Brak in that awful moment as he stood before her. Finally, shuddering, he lowered his sword.

"Let them go," he said.

Nordica smiled. "I will. That is my bargain."

"No, by the lords of war!" Pemma bawled. "Even though it means my father's life, I cannot stand by like a coward and—*Brak!*"

The barbarian had dropped his sword in the dust. He turned and walked toward the castle gates.

"*Brak!*" Pemma shouted again.

The barbarian never turned.

Walking without feeling, Brak passed between the high gates he had struggled so hard to open. Pemma's last entreaty died away beneath the wail of the wind. Nordica's merry laugh sounded a moment later as she followed with Scarletjaw at heel.

Failure overwhelmed Brak then. Dimmed his mind, brutalized his senses. He heard the gates creak shut. He

150

heard the massive oaken bar drop into place. Then, horror on horror, he heard Nordica's voice, strong and commanding:

"To the ramparts, archers! Kill them both before they flee. A silver purse apiece to the two men whose arrows strike down Pemma and Strann. For the glory of the Dark One!"

At once the courtyard was utter confusion. Archers scrambled up ladders. And Brak went berserk, swinging around like a great blind beast until he sighted Nordica near the gate.

Arrows whicked and whispered on the wind. "Lying slut!" Brak roared. "You swore—"

"*My lady!*"

Nordica whipped her head up. "A hit?"

The man shouted from the battlements: "Both Strann and his son are fallen with arrows through their bodies."

"Slut from hell!" Brak was screaming, running at Nordica. "Devil-spawned woman!"

Men converged upon him from all sides. They clubbed him, kicked him. They held his shoulders, his arms, his legs while he fought wildly. Blow after blow struck his skull.

Into his mind drifted the weird sound of howling wind. It was mixed with the shrieking laughter of a woman:

"*Too late, Brak, too late. I have waited for this hour. Waited and yearned for it ever since you turned your face from me in the Ice-marches and sent me to limbo with my father's dagger in my back. His thaumaturgical skills and the might of Yob-Haggoth brought me back to serve the Dark One again. And tonight the power comes full circle.*"

"Ariane?" he bellowed in delirium. "You *are* Ariane—!"

"*Yes, yes! And tonight I summon the four winds and change metal into gold by taking your life. My father Septegundus said the words to you. I WILL BE THERE. IT WAS NOT AN IDLE THREAT!*"

Then the blows of the soldiers brought total dark.

Chapter XII

LEAD INTO GOLD, DEAD INTO LIVING

—*awake, awake, awake, awake, awake.*

The voice beat, echoed, sang far away. It pulsed loud one moment, then diminished in the next.

Brak grumbled to himself. He tried to find a way out of the thick, chill darkness which seemed to wrap him. He grew aware of restraints on his arms. He opened his eyes.

The blackness vanished. The soldier holding Brak from behind repeated, "Lady? The yellow-haired one is awake."

And memory swept back.

The strange keening echo of a moment before had been the guard's words bouncing within the hollow of his semiconscious mind. Slowly he straightened, glanced around. The wind buffeted him. His belly knotted as he saw where he was, and with whom.

The chamber was large and round. It was open all around its circumference. A series of arches led onto a portico that circled the room. Through one of the arches Brak glimpsed mountain peaks, sharp in the day's graying light.

The chamber had a feeling of spaciousness, of airiness and great height. He realized that it had to be located somewhere near the top of the castle, for the perspective of the mountains was different than it had been from the courtyard.

The wind came whipping through the arches. Here and there gusts of it seemed to congeal, coalesce into faint but discernible milky clouds.

These clouds disappeared almost the instant they formed. But they suggested that the currents of air boiling

152

into the chamber possessed some awful supernatural life of their own.

Brak got another powerful shock when he noticed that each of the pillars supporting the arches contained a small niche. In each niche, stone eyes watching, stone fists clenched in malevolent fury, stone mouth turned downward like a fisher's hook—in each niche, an image of Yob-Haggoth.

Upon the rough-hewn stone floor a great circle had been marked out in chalky white. Peculiar crosses were positioned on its rim at four equidistant points. One of these crosses was chalked directly in front of Brak's feet.

Directly across from him on the other side of the circle was another such mark. Standing behind it, not bound as Brak was bound, but guarded by a trio of soldiers who held spears ready at his back, was Runga.

The smith's flesh wound had been bound up with linen. His eyes were dull with fright.

To Brak's left, where another cross was drawn, old Darios the seaman tottered. His beard flapped in the wind. He was likewise guarded by three men. And on the barbarian's right, Elinor was held captive by a similar trio.

All at once Brak understood the dreadful meaning of the ring and the cross-marks with their human counterparts.

The four sacrifices stood in a representation of the circle of creation, each at a point from which blew one of the four winds of the earth.

In the center of the ring a block of stone formed a low dais. Around this dais and radiating outward to the ring's perimeter, a convoluted maze of mystic symbols had been sketched.

As Brak vainly tried to decipher the various pentagrams and star-shapes, he heard a rustling above the beat of the winds.

Nordica appeared, face white as her virginal gown.

Her hair blew out behind her, a blood-colored banner. She was barefoot, strangely expressionless. In her hands she carried a small bar of gray metal.

She proceeded slowly to the center of the ring. She laid the bar on the dais and gazed down at it.

Nordica's gown danced around her supple calves,

blown first one way, then another as the winds howled louder and louder still.

Slowly her head came up.

She turned. She looked at Brak. The scarlet lips curved ever so slightly. They said more than words ever could.

On those lips Brak saw Ariane's smile of victory and revenge.

Nordica's jade eyes were oddly opaque. Brak felt an immense, sinking helplessness as that calm stare enveloped him.

Ariane had won. He knew it. She no longer had to reveal herself to him to prove that it was so.

Here and there Brak saw again the pearlescent eddies, like air-borne waves, as the winds seemed to take tangible form. Runga began to whimper.

One of the smith's guards cuffed him in the side of the head. The disturbance seemed to shatter Nordica's calm. She glared. The guards seized Runga to keep him from staggering forward into the ring.

Brak swiped at his eyes. His bonds restrained him but did not stifle all motion. There was an incredible weariness in him; an ache in both his body and his mind; a futility born of too many battles against impossible odds.

Runga quieted. Brak dared to look at Elinor.

She was trembling as Runga had trembled. But at least she made an effort to hold herself proudly in spite of it.

The lead bar shone ominously on the dais.

Only Darios the seaman did not see it. His cheeks were still flushed with fever. He was propped up by the hands of the guards assigned to watch him.

Nordica lifted her right hand. She pointed beyond an arch at the peaks and the sky.

When she spoke, it was with the barest movement of her lips. Yet Brak heard her clearly despite the shriek of the wind that blew so violently that the guards had trouble standing erect. They, in fact, leaned slightly in order to maintain their balance. Only Nordica seemed untouched by the storm-force.

"In the exalted name of Yob-Haggoth the Dark One I invoke the four winds," Nordica said, finger extended to the boiling sky. *"The four winds in conjunction bring the*

power. The four winds from the ends of time, from the ends of creation, from the black abyss beyond the edge of life where dwells dark my Lord—the four winds COME!"

A gust whipped into the open chamber. Brak thought he felt the solid floor sway.

"Yob-Haggoth send the north wind!" Nordica sang. *"Send the blue north wind's chill!"*

Through the open archway behind Runga, wind screamed and moaned.

Brak felt a frosty breath on his chest. The chamber seemed to swim in a blue-tinted mist.

Nordica cried:

"Yob-Haggoth send the south wind! Send the green wind of the heat that decays!"

A belching-hot gust of hot air seethed into the chamber, ripe with the stink of vegetation dead for a century in some sodden rain-forest. One of the guards behind Brak began to vomit.

"Yob-Haggoth send the east wind! Send the red wind's poppy poison!"

Elinor and her guards swayed as the wind poured through the arch behind them, ripe with a cloying, sickening sweetness.

"Yob-Haggoth send the west wind! Send the black wind's voice from land's end!"

Darios and his captors vanished in a swirling cloud of inky air. The cloud crawled and crept and leaped toward the central dais. Suddenly the entire chamber seemed to be caught in a whirlpool gale.

Strange patches of color danced before Brak's eyes. Above him, in the center of the multicolor fume, an image began to form—

A shaven pate.

An aquiline nose.

Thin, pitiless lips—

Brak's heart pounded in his huge chest. Fear, then. *Fear*—

Eyes formed in the wind-whirl, large, dark, with immense pupils. Pads of scar tissue wrinkled like a pus-filled crust above the eyes as they fixed Brak with an inhumanly triumphant stare—

The face materialized around the features. Brak saw the

155

skin alive and crawling with intertwined human figures in awful postures of pain.

Out of the storm-boil the eyes turned toward him.

Septegundus, Amyr of Evil upon Earth, saw Brak's torment, and his phantom face said the torment was good.

Then, as the hideous dance of tortured figures within the face continued slowly and slowly, the glaring eyes looked elsewhere in the wind-mist—

Septegundus, Amyr of Evil upon Earth, saw the work of his daughter Ariane, and his phantom face said the work was good.

The wind-clouds turned and howled with glee. In the sound Brak heard Septegundus merrily mocking him. Mocking him with laughter that welcomed him finally and inevitably into the hands of Yob-Haggoth, into the blasphemous god's thrice-fired hells—

And a voice seemed to thunder—

I WILL BE THERE!

*　*　*

Savagely Brak squeezed his eyes shut. When he looked again, only Nordica stood in the center of the maelstrom. Her gown was unruffled. Her hair was undisturbed.

Both hands raised, Nordica spun toward the big barbarian.

"*To the glory of Yob-Haggoth—couple the south wind with the earth—breathe the gold alive!*"

In his legs Brak felt a tingling.

The tingling became acute pain.

The pain rose swiftly through his entire body, until he was enveloped by a vast, numbing hurt.

Nordica turned to Darios.

"*To the glory of Yob-Haggoth—couple the west wind with the water—breathe the gold alive!*"

Darios shrieked, clutched his chest. His frail body seemed to wilt and shrink.

"*To the glory of Yob-Haggoth—couple the north wind with the fire—breathe the gold alive!*"

Runga was sobbing. Tears ran down his cheeks as he shuddered, clenched his fists at his sides.

"*To the glory of Yob-Haggoth—couple the east wind*

with the air—BREATHE THE GOLD ALIVE!"

Elinor moaned and would have pitched forward had not one of the frightened guards seized her.

"Earth! Air! Fire! Water! Gather, creation! Gather, winds! BLOW AND BURN AND BREATHE THE GOLD ALIVE!"

Brak felt more enfeebled with every moment that passed. His head pounded. His eyes misted. His legs were weak as an infant's, and he wondered how long he could stand erect.

Then, as if Nordica had magically wished understanding upon him, some still-sharpened corner of his mind gave him the answer.

The dull gray bar on the murky dais was beginning to emit a faint yellow radiance.

As though a kind of life were being drawn into it.

And at the same time, he knew that life was being drained out of his own body, being sucked and pulled and torn out by the raging, raging winds—

Like sand trickling down in an hourglass, the strength left his muscles. He no longer felt that he had bones, but that he was instead a creature made of a jellyish marrow. When the last drop of his life had been taken, he would be limp, dead, a slimed spot on the rock floor.

It was happening to the other three captives as well.

They seemed to grow smaller and more pale. The winds had darkened, become almost a fog. The chamber swayed more violently. Brak thought he heard a far-off rumbling, as though the very foundations of the castle were being rocked.

He struggled to keep his head up. He saw a jagged fissure open in the stone of the arch above and behind Runga.

A guard cursed somewhere. The man had seen the fissure too, and guessed the threat the winds posed.

But Nordica's cheeks shone yellow in the mounting glow from the bar on the dais, and she saw nothing else.

"Winds, take life from the living! Winds, breathe life into dead matter! Winds, seize life from the fire and air, the earth and water and change base lead to burning gold so that the dominion of Yob-Haggoth shall know no end!"

Brighter pulsed the lead bar.
Brighter.

It became streaked and dappled with bright yellow patches as first one section, then another, began to alter.

Nordica leaned over the bar, her hands like claws. Her voice was lost suddenly in the ripping, howling fury of the wind that had become a tornado, a mating of the breaths of heaven into one ferocious scream of strength.

Brak had the sensation that he was falling. He knew it was only because the life was leaving his body, somehow drawn across the chamber to feed into that shining bar. Beyond all hope, he knew he was finished, and the others too.

Yet some wild, savage will to live, some bowel-deep instinct born into him on the high steppes, refused to succumb. His foggy mind ran blindly through passage after passage, hunting escape, escape, or even some weapon to destroy himself and Nordi—no, no! *Ariane!*

He was too enfeebled to fight. The hell-winds gripped him like immense hands. He had very little time left.

But to bow down—to let his life-stuff be drained into a metal bar and that bar used to buy more lives, more souls, more power for the Dark One—*NO!*

Slowly, sinuously, Nordica Fire-Hair began to move around the dais. Her hands formed signs Brak did not understand. Her mouth worked, repeating words. Brak heard none of them. The only sound was the shriek of the winds pouring through the arches, sweeping and storming around and around in the maelstrom of force.

Dimly he perceived that the sky outside had darkened. From far below, the castle foundations ground and rumbled again—

In that moment Brak's straining mind remembered.

He remembered because he was cursing the first day he had ridden—been forced to ride—into this bewitched kingdom.

He remembered a cry in the Manworm pit.

He remembered how he had almost failed to save Elinor.

He remembered how strength had poured into his arm.

And he remembered the source of that strength, and a

158

mind which roamed far beyond its own boundaries.

Brak's lips twisted grotesquely. Down in that pit, Celsus Hyrcanus still lived.

Mad, yes.

But alive.

And Nordica—if any part of Nordica still existed in the mind and body which Ariane had seized—*did not know.*

* * *

Ambrose?

Brak tried to reach out with his mind. Tried to grasp the image of the old man perched on the pillar with the peculiar stone cross hung on a chain around his neck.

Ambrose? Ambrose?

The wind howled, battering Brak's body like a physical blow.

Ambrose? Ambrose? Reach here. Reach me. WHERE ARE YOU?

Then, feebly, very distant, in a language without words, he heard:

Here.

* * *

The pain, the enervating lifelessness that had gripped him seemed to retreat a little. Nordica's figure, sweeping and turning around the dais where the bar glowed bright yellow, seemed indistinct. In a featureless limbo of black cold, of pure mind, Brak sought Ambrose the Pillarite, crying:

Help us. If you truly have the power of your Nameless God, help us before we die and she and her father ride their power like a stallion over the earth.

Cool and faint, the voice without words answered from far off:

The strength of the Nameless God is mine. I will try. Ask.

In the pit—the Manworm pit—

Brak had difficulty maintaining the contact. He was reaching into a frightening void whose nature he did not understand.

159

—an old man lives. Witless. Half dead. Bring him here. Move him as you or your god's power moved my arm that first day. Lift him and bring him here to this chamber before we all die.

The answer rang back, so ferocious that Brak felt as though a fire-needle had been driven into his skull:

No! That is too much. My power is required also. And I am old. I cannot lift him, nor send him that distance.

Nordica's incantation had become a shrill, steady scream beating above the wind. Runga was slumped on his knees, hands clasped in prayer as his life drained away. Darios had already succumbed. He lay on his back, mouth open. Elinor hung in the grip of her terrified guards. Apart from an occasional bob of her head, she too seemed lifeless.

The chamber began to fill with a blinding yellow light. It was hurtful to the eye. The life-stuff of each sacrifice poured faster into the bar upon the dais, *faster—*

Bring the alchemist! Brak's brain cried out across the fathomless void of mind. *Try, mystic! Clutch your cross! Pray! Beg your god if he must be begged. But try! Else the powers of evil will sweep from this chamber to the ends of the world!*

The echoing answer came:

I have not the strength.

And Brak shrieked with all his being:

Try before the darkness falls! TRY!

Suddenly the sharp, cold limbo through which he had been forcing his mind—vanished.

Brak felt weak as before. Listless. Each limb was heavy, growing heavier.

He had lost the contact.

Ambrose?

AMBROSE?

Silently he cried the mystic's name. His thoughts met a wall of pain past which he could not reach. A low, savage moan of despair left his lips. He abandoned himself to the draining of the winds.

Another fissure opened in an arch behind Elinor. It was wider than the first. Dust powdered down.

One of the soldiers tried to shout a warning to Nordica. She did not hear. She was lost in her obscene, contorted ritual, whirling and turning around the transmuting bar, her body an animated gold statue in the reflected light.

Beneath Brak's feet the stone shook again. Even as he wondered how long the chamber would survive, a new bolt of pain speared into his belly. He threw back his head, screamed aloud.

The guards backed away from him, huddling together. Brak fell to his knees. He pounded his temples as the hurt beat higher inside him.

Through the mistiness of the wind-clouds he saw Nordica's golden face crack into a smile.

And her eyes were dark.

Ariane's.

The pain in Brak doubled—

Trebled.

Trebled again—

Then suddenly his mind broke the wall again, and he heard Ambrose's voiceless cry:

He will come. Though I die, he will come. The Nameless God wills it. The pain burns me. Tortures me. Yet he is coming from the pit. Be ready! THE AL-CHEMIST IS COMING—

"Woman?" Brak yelled. He dragged himself across the edge of the ring. "Nordica—Ariane—witch-woman —whatever you call yourself—listen to me!"

Seeing Brak lurch toward her, she cried orders to the soldiers. He didn't hear.

Within his temples beat a wave of power that rose higher and higher, counterbalancing the draining, leeching force of the winds.

Brak forgot the soldiers who struggled with their own terror and tried to force their numbed limbs to move and obey the commands. The floor of the chamber was opening now, great cracks splitting it, intersecting one another. A keystone in one of the outer arches dropped with a thunderous crash.

"Woman?" Brak shrieked. "Witch-woman? Your magic is worthless! Mine is stronger—" The pain-wave beat higher in him, unbearably close to a climax. "I will raise the dead, woman! I will bring the ghost of one you slew out of lust and greed—"

White fire exploded behind Brak's eyes. For a moment he saw nothing.

Then the winds died completely.

* * *

Nordica's voice rang out, wordless, terrified. Brak's eyes flew open.

There, beside the dais where the yellow bar was dulling again, streaked with gray, streaked with black—*there*—

An amorphous whiteness congealed into a torso—

Into legs—

Into all four limbs—

Far away Brak heard Ambrose the Pillarite's whimper of mind-pain. The figure of Celsus Hyrcanus materialized.

Nordica shrieked. "Father! My father Septegundus —help me!"

The mad old alchemist muttered, "Where—where—?" His head was turning, turning. All at once his eyes fell on Nordica's face.

The barriers of madness crumbled in an instant. The cracked old tongue licked at the ancient lips and Celsus Hyrcanus was wholly sane:

"Nordica! My flesh. My flesh of evil. My own flesh that tried to kill me—is it you?"

The old, watering lids blinked, blinked again. "There is something, Nordica—ah! Your eyes. They're not—not my daughter's. I—yes! I recognize that look—"

A shuffling step forward. "I saw it just before you tried to destroy me, girl. But you aren't my girl any longer, just my flesh. *Then who is it inside you?"*

Hands outstretched like claws, a real, a solid Celsus Hyrcanus lunged for his daughter's throat.

Nordica cried the name of Septegundus again. Her wild howl drowned in a thunderclap of sound.

The lead bar on the dais cracked in half.

In the seconds that followed the rolling, ear-splitting boom, the bar collapsed to dust and the four winds crashed together in the center of the chamber where for an instant the body of Celsus Hyrcanus had held them at bay. Somewhere a pained voice—Ambrose?—moaned with sudden relief.

162

In the aftermath of the thunderclap Brak was running, back toward his guards. From one, with new strength that split his bonds, he grappled a spear.

He spun around, half-crouched, no longer a man but an animal, teeth bared, face inhuman. Stones began to drop from the arch where the keystone had fallen.

The floor of the chamber tilted. Other arches began to crack and crumble. Even as Brak raced toward Elinor he saw a great stone fall, smashing a soldier and poor, feeble Darios to red smears beneath it.

Another soldier trying to escape crossed Brak's path near the rim of the chalk ring. He lopped wildly at the barbarian with his sword. Brak rammed the spear into the man's guts, yanked it out, then rushed on.

He reached Elinor. He dragged her up from the floor where she'd fallen. He slung the girl over his shoulder and ran toward what looked like a stairway entrance.

The winds were battering at the chamber. Stone after stone crashed down. A moment more and the entire structure would topple.

Brak heard nothing but the steady thunder of falling masonry mingled with the tormented, orgiastic cry of the tornado-force winds. He stumbled against someone, saw that it was Runga—

The burly smith hammered at the barbarian with his fists, trying to get ahead down the stairs. Encumbered by the shepherd girl over his shoulder, Brak still managed to bring his spear around and thrust it deep into Runga's belly.

The smith cried out, pitched backward, carrying the spear with him. Blood fountained warm and sticky onto Brak's shoulder.

Another soldier rushed by, tripped on the first stair and went tumbling into the dark below. His cry was sharp and awful.

Brak raced down that stair between walls of stone that seemed like silken hangings so violently did they sway and tremble. At a turning on the staircase he found the guard who had fallen. The man's neck was broken. Brak snatched up the soldier's broadsword and plunged on.

The stair seemed to wind downward forever. Brak was

growing weaker by the second. He felt Elinor stir against him. At last, light gleamed ahead.

Near to crying from relief at this sight, Brak burst through a door onto a rampart that led along the castle wall. At the rampart's far end a ladder led down to the main courtyard. From there it was not far to the great gates through which Nordica's soldiers were fleeing like panicked beasts.

Brak halted long enough to put Elinor on her feet. He held her until she regained her balance and her senses.

"Can you walk, girl? We're nearly free——"

"I can walk. Take my hand. That's all the help I need."

"We must hurry. The winds around the tower may destroy all of this place before they're done."

Brak's last words were muffled by another loud roar. He turned toward the high stone tower at whose top he could dimly discern the arched chamber half-hidden in clouds of mist.

That chamber, and the entire top of the tower, were falling outward, into the gorge beyond the castle.

"She's done. Buried and done, and her magic with her," Brak breathed, not truly knowing in this chaos of noise and horror whether he meant Nordica, or Ariane, or both. "We've come through it alive, girl."

And he clasped Elinor's hand and began to run.

They had gone halfway down the rampart when the stench swept over them.

Brak skidded to a halt again, whipped around. His heart broke with defeat.

Down the rampart, out of the same door through which they had escaped, eyes bright as moons and white fangs shining, ran Scarletjaw.

Brak's only weapon was the broadsword in his fist. And it would be totally useless against the hound's armored skin.

"Beast!"

The cry made Brak turn around again.

"Beast, take them!"

There in the courtyard stood Nordica.

Or was it?

He recognized the white gown. It was flowered with the

blood that leaked from her shattered ribs, from her ripped throat, from her crushed thigh. He recognized the copper hair turned filthy by mortar dust. How the—*woman? creature? thing?*—had escaped from the tower he did not precisely know. Yet he sensed she had come from there; been crushed and broken there, only to rise.

With some of the blood on her gown belonging to Celsus Hyrcanus? Probably.

Brak's mouth was hot and sour. Even as he watched, the stained and filthy cheeks of that face seemed to peel away. He saw again the dazzling illusion of a bony skull.

Then it too blurred. He saw a new face with plum lips, dark eyes intense as hell's own ovens—

An unblemished and beautiful face.

Ariane.

Behind her, darkening, swelling, rose a fire-tinged cloud from which the crawling face of Septegundus looked out.

Ariane's beautiful lips peeled back in a ghastly smile as she watched the dog lope straight at Brak.

The big barbarian stared at the blade in his hand. It could not help him.

Elinor began to sob mindlessly. Brak knew this was the last battle.

The sword in his fist shone like tin. Swiping his forearm across his eyes to clear them, he threw it away.

Some dim comprehension of what Brak had done penetrated Elinor's terrorized mind. She started babbling senselessly, telling him of his mistake. But he paid scant heed, readying himself for Scarletjaw's lunge as the beast gathered speed.

Elinor cried more loudly, cursing him in her fright. She reviled him for throwing away their sole chance for survival—

Scarletjaw left the rampart, leaped high, hurtled through the air, great claws questing, great jaws open.

Brak the barbarian knew his hour had struck. But he did not run away. He was a berserker now. He meant to die slaughtering.

He ran in beneath the belly of the beast as it hurtled down. He thrust upward with both hands. He bit his lips until blood gushed as the monstrous weight of the animal fell upon him.

But he was ready for one last push. He gave it, upward, upward and out with all his might.

Talons raked his back, his flanks, his spine, until he thought it would crack. He pushed harder. Higher. *Harder. Higher—*

Then Scarletjaw was tumbling through the air; Brak had lifted and thrown him from the rampart down into the courtyard below.

Numbly Brak leaned on the battlement. The great hound struck the earth, twitched. Then the monster rose shakily.

"Beast?" came the witch-woman's astonished voice. "My beautiful beast. You had all of Yob-Haggoth's power and still he killed y—*no!*"

Scarletjaw smelled the blood on Nordica's gown.

Slowly, left hind leg dragging, the animal hitched himself forward.

Nordica turned to run. She stumbled.

Scarletjaw leaped.

Nordica-with-the-face-of-Ariane let out a single cry. Perhaps it was her father's name she screamed. Perhaps it was Yob-Haggoth's. The swirling fire-tinged cloud roiled, started to sweep down around her, protectively.

But it was far too late. The legs of the bleeding woman carried her away from the cloud. She staggered one step.

Staggered another.

Stumbled.

Scarletjaw leaped.

Brak seized Elinor's hand, dragged her head against his chest, held it down.

There was one more high and piercing scream.

Then a crack-crunch of bones.

The blood of the body that had belonged to Nordica Fire-Hair ran like a river in the courtyard.

* * *

Holding Elinor so that she could not see, Brak stared as the body tumbled over and over and over, ripped into gory sections by the fangs of the immense dog. The fire-bellied black cloud in which he thought he glimpsed the baleful eyes of Septegundus descended close to the corpse.

166

From the corpse a tiny wisping curl leaped up like smoke. It melted into the cloud.

Somewhere a laugh rang out. A woman's laugh, cruel, mocking.

The cloud rumbled. It flickered with internal fires and swallowed the crawling face of the Amyr of Evil upon Earth into itself.

Nordica lay dead.

But somehow Ariane the Daughter of Hell, aided by her father's sorcerous might, had fled the corpse at the last instant. She lived still. Temporarily defeated, true. But only temporarily.

The dark cloud ripped apart and diffused into the morning air and was gone.

* * *

Without quite remembering how they accomplished it, Brak and Elinor reached the ladder leading down to the floor of the courtyard near the gate. They stole out through the open doors. Once on the road, they began to run hand in hand.

Before they had gone far, the earth shook under them. Brak spun.

All the upper towers of Nordica's keep were lost in whirling wind-driven murk. Slowly they appeared, breaking, falling, collapsing in upon themselves one by one, crumbling in upon Nordica's corpse, and Scarletjaw, and the idols of Yob-Haggoth, and all the immense evil of the place.

Crumbling—crumbling and destroying all—

All but Ariane—

And Septegundus.

In Brak's mind the words rang fearsomely.

I WILL BE THERE.

The promise was reborn with added meaning.

* * *

As Brak and the shepherd girl now trudged on down the road toward a group of Nordica's soldiers, weaponless and

168

no longer hostile, the barbarian felt that he was so tired he might never walk again.

They reached the soldiers. The men made no move to harm the pair, merely stared in sullen silence. The wind beat loud in Brak's ears.

He took one last look at the accursed castle. Under the battering of the winds from the ends of the earth, it was settling into a mammoth pile of rubble.

Nordica Fire-Hair's cairn.

But not Ariane's.

* * *

Several days later, in clear sunlight, Brak the barbarian mounted a pony in the yard of the palace of Strann, Lord of The Silver Balances.

At Brak's flank hung a new broadsword. Nearby stood Prince Pemma, now Lord Pemma. The young ruler's new position was symbolized by an ivory diadem that somehow lent his plain, pleasant features a more regal cast. But those features were grave.

At Pemma's side stood Elinor. She was bathed, perfumed, freshly-clothed and nearly recovered from her ordeal. Prince Pemma had insisted that she, as well as Ambrose the Pillarite, be housed in the palace until they recovered. Ambrose remained in a near-coma, from time to time muttering oblique praise to his Nameless God.

Pemma strode forward. His doublet bulged slightly beneath his left arm because of the layers of linen wrappings the physicians had applied. Nordica's archers had slain Strann, whose body lay in state in the palace chapel. But the arrow piercing Pemma's back had not sped true. The young man had lived to assume his father's crown.

Brak fingered the fine silver bosses of the riding gear which Pemma had provided.

"I will stay, Lord," he said to the young man, "if the doctors are still not sure of the Pillarite's fate. I owe him much."

And his god? Of that, Brak was uncertain.

"No, we will care for him," Pemma answered. "Al-

169

though the physicians don't understand the exact nature of his sickness—how can they when his mind may have been damaged forever by his struggle to destroy Nordica and save you?—they are still reasonably confident that he will survive. Regardless of what hurt has been done to him, he'll have a safe, secure place of honor in my household. Until his dying day if he wishes it."

From the ranks of royal troops drawn up in their armor around the yard, Iskander marched forward.

"I for one would welcome it if you'd remain, barbarian. I could use a strong fighting arm—an aide with your courage. The pay would be handsome and the life pleasant—now that she's gone."

Brak shook his head. "I'm still bound south. To Khurdisan." His eyes roamed the horizon uneasily for a moment, watching.

Suddenly Elinor broke away from the young lord's side. She rushed up beside the barbarian's pony, seized his hand. Though she kept her eyes averted, there was an unmistakable color in her cheeks.

"Many times I've thanked you, Brak. But ten thousand wouldn't be enough." She raised her head to look at him. "Perhaps if you remained there would be fortunes to find here."

What he saw through her natural shyness was the beginning of an emotion that, somehow, stung his heart. She made a lovely figure in the sunlight. Then he thought of Queen Rhea, left behind in Phrixos.

Sighing, with his other hand Brak reached down to touch her hand clasped over his.

"Girl, I'm not a man for a court or a king's house. I'll ride to the end of the earth before I'm done, probably. It was in my blood to do it when I was born. I—"

He noticed Prince Pemma observing the exchange closely. The young monarch had a peculiar expression on his face.

The Prince was jealous!

Brak smiled then. Truly smiled for the first time in many days. Well Pemma might be jealous. Outfitted properly, this was a handsome wench.

Carefully Brak drew his hand from Elinor's.

170

"Now that Nordica's evil no longer infests the land, the young lord will make a fine ruler, girl. When I'm gone, perhaps your eye will look on him differently. Perhaps one day you might even find life in a palace preferable to loneliness on the high slope. At least," he added with a gleam in his eye, "it's worthy of your thought."

Startled, Elinor glanced at Pemma. She flushed even more deeply before she glanced away.

Pemma smiled in return. Then he grew grave once more:

"You still have not answered my prime question, barbarian."

"Even though you've pressed it on me every hour since we came down from that hell's keep," he grumbled, shifting on the pony's back. The trappings jingled. The pony stamped and blew, spirited, anxious to be away.

"At the gates," said Pemma, "you called Nordica by another name."

"I was out of my head," Brak replied, too quickly. "Surely you can understand. The confusion of the moment—"

"You said," Pemma persisted, "that she served that god called the Dark One. You were quite coherent, Brak."

"I tell you I was out of my senses!"

"Foreknowledge is a wise defense, Brak. I need to know about her. I need to be prepared, should she ever come back to haunt me."

"It's not you she'll haunt," Brak said with another grim glance to the south.

"As Lord here, barbarian, I demand that you explain how—"

Brak dug his knees into his mount's flanks. "Take me south, pony."

While Pemma hallooed and waved after him, Brak rode out through the gate under the tower where the Doomsbell hung silent.

He galloped down through the pleasant vineyards where the peasants labored again in the sunlight. They were turning earth and planting new vines to replace the ones that had been burned.

He heard the peasants singing a work-song. Their

171

voices were lusty. The music cheered him a little. He followed the road to its next bending.

The bending led south.

With a final glance at the horizon, he shrugged and turned his pony's head toward whatever lay in wait.

BRAK #1: The Barbarian
By John Jakes

PRICE: $2.25   T51650
CATEGORY: Science Fiction/Fantasy

BRAK—The Barbarian

BRAK, a magnificent epic series of science fiction and fantasy in a savage age of blood and barbarism. BRAK, the mighty yellow-haired warrior, on a journey through strange kingdoms and dark perils of foul sorcery. BRAK, with dazzling broadsword in hand, battles grotesque evils as he travels his fated path!

COMING IN THE BRAK SERIES BY JOHN JAKES:
  BRAK #2: THE MARK OF THE DEMONS
  BRAK #3: THE SORCERESS
  BRAK #4: WHEN THE IDOLS WALKED

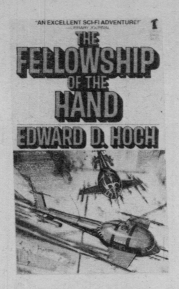

THE FELLOWSHIP OF THE HAND
By Edward D. Hoch

PRICE: $1.75   T51606
CATEGORY: Science Fiction